SWEET APPLE CHRISTMAS

A HEARTSPRINGS VALLEY WINTER TALE (BOOK 3)

ANNE CHASE

THOMAS PUBLISHING

ISBN-13: 978-1945320118

For Gavin, Haley, Robert, and Luc

CHAPTER 1

*H*olly stepped briskly down the path that wound along the shore of Heartsprings Lake, her boots crunching on the fresh snow underfoot. What a gorgeous afternoon! She breathed in deeply, enjoying the crisp air filling her lungs. She hadn't been sure about the weather that morning — the blustery winds she'd encountered on her five a.m. walk to the cafe were hardly encouraging — but Mother Nature had chosen to bestow something lovely upon her small town: a beautiful winter afternoon.

She inhaled again and caught a hint of evergreen from the forest blanketing the surrounding ridge. Sunlight glinted off the ice-covered lake, punctuated by flashes of light from the blades of the skaters dashing to and fro. Her eyes were drawn to a child of four or five, anxious parents in tow, taking her first tentative steps on skates, her little legs moving awkwardly but with determination. Farther out, a group of older kids, hockey sticks in hand, passed a puck back and forth, shouting encouragement to one another.

In the distance, a man was skating quickly and assuredly across the ice, really pushing himself, like he was in training. She squinted through the sun's bright glare. Did she know him? Had she seen him before? Hard to tell, given the distance. He moved like a hockey player — smooth and graceful, with controlled power and purpose. Like he was working out and enjoying himself while doing so.

Kind of like her, with her brisk power walk. Her daily forty-five-minute break from work. Her chance to get out of the cafe after the lunch rush died down, to breathe in fresh air and clear her head, to recharge body and soul and give her the energy to push through the rest of her day. When the weather was nice, like today, her walk took her from Heartsprings Valley's town square through her adorable neighborhood to the shores of the small lake. In twenty-two minutes, if she maintained a fast pace, she could reach this very spot and take in the beauty of the landscape. The view that greeted her changed with the seasons — flowers in the spring, tall grasses in the summer, gorgeous red leaves in the fall — but she'd always been most partial to winter, when snow blanketed the hills and her fellow townspeople bundled themselves up and headed out onto the ice, their faces sporting rosy cheeks and big smiles.

Yes, this time of year was definitely the best, with snow a recent arrival and Christmas right around the corner. Her favorite holiday always seemed to bring a bounce in her step, a lift in her spirits, a twinkle in her eye, a — *oh, stop that!* she told herself. All these peppy clichés running through her head — she was starting to sound like her mom, who tossed off cheery homilies as easily as she breathed. She loved her mom dearly, but sometimes her unbridled optimism was a bit exasperating. Sometimes, being realistic was what mattered most.

She picked up her pace. Even without looking at the watch under the glove covering her left wrist, she knew it was time to turn around and head back. There were so many things to do: Dough to make for more scones. Orders to box up. Customers to serve.

A cookbook to finish…. A sigh escaped her lips. She was so close to finishing her labor of love, yet so far. Something was missing — she knew that — but she didn't know what….

Lost in thought, she didn't hear at first the voice calling her name.

"Holly! Hello, Holly! Young lady!"

She stopped in her tracks as the words "young lady" managed to register. She wasn't young anymore, not really — thirty-eight was awfully close to forty — but it was nice to be addressed that way.

She turned to see Bert Winters, the mayor of Heartsprings Valley, bounding up from the edge of the lake.

"Bert, I'm so sorry," she said as he approached. "I was stuck in my head."

"Glad I ran into you," Bert said, huffing and puffing a bit. "Whoa, these old lungs aren't what they used to be." He paused to catch his breath and Holly hid a smile. Bert hinted all the time that he was getting too old to keep doing what he did, but he wasn't fooling her or anyone else — he had more energy than most people she knew. With his white hair and beard, shrewd eyes and unbridled enthusiasm for all things Heartsprings Valley, he looked like Santa's younger brother.

"What brings you out here today?" she asked.

Bert gestured to the group of kids passing the hockey puck on the ice. "Grandson and his friends."

"Those kids?" she said, pointing to them. "That gaggle of speed demons?"

"Every time I blink, they get bigger and faster."

"How can I help you?"

"It's about the charity drive," Bert said. "Checking to see where we are."

She nodded. As one of the organizers for the town's annual Christmas charity drive, she'd been tracking their fundraising progress closely. "We're doing well — up a bit compared to last year — but still have a ways to go."

"What's your gut telling you?" he asked her, his eyes searching her face. "Are we going to reach our goal?"

No, she almost said, but stopped herself. As important as it was to be realistic about challenges, she'd learned to be cautious about expressing doubt. Even when people said they wanted to "keep it real," they usually preferred to "keep it vaguely hopeful."

"The drive runs for another week," she said instead. "We'll see."

Bert's brow furrowed. Every Christmas, local businesses in Heartsprings Valley — including the cafe Holly owned and managed on the town square — joined together to support worthy causes. This year's drive was for a cause close to Bert's heart: support for military veterans and their families.

"Let me do some noodling," Bert said. "Talk to the wife and a few others — get some ideas."

"Anything I can do, you let me know."

"Will do. Oh, and I'll be by later for my order."

Holly smiled. "More maple scones?"

He chuckled and patted his stomach. "Never been able to resist 'em. See you in a bit."

CHAPTER 2

*N*ineteen minutes later, Holly cracked open the back door of her cafe and stepped into the kitchen, a smile lighting up her face as the familiar sights and scents and sounds greeted her — the freshly cooked spinach quiche cooling on the counter, the fried potatoes on the grill, the sizzle of bacon in a pan. The kitchen was large and airy, with two ovens and a grill along one wall, three big refrigerator-freezers along another, and a deep sink and dishwasher along a third. Along the back wall, a bank of tall windows filled the room with afternoon light. In the center of the room, a stainless-steel island provided plenty of prep space. Tucked next to the back door was a well-stocked pantry, along with a small desk that served as the cafe's de-facto business headquarters.

Her line cook, George — a rough-and-tumble guy

in his sixties — looked up from the bacon strips he was crisping. "How was the lake, boss?" He was a burly man with short-cropped graying hair and a face custom-built for scowling.

"Beautiful," she replied as she hung up her coat on the rack next to the door and took off her scarf and gloves. As expected, the mail had arrived while she was out. She flipped through the stack on her desk and smiled when she found two Christmas cards, which she promptly opened. The first, from a regular patron of the cafe, depicted a snowy winter mountain at night overlooking a tiny town glowing with warm lights, along with the words, "Comfort and Joy." She opened the second card and chuckled at the sight of her friend Ted, owner of the local hardware store, and his fiancée Peggy, dressed up as Santa and Mrs. Claus. They had big grins on their faces and were clearly enjoying themselves. Along the bottom of the photo were the words, "Ho ho ho! Merry Christmas from Cane Hardware!"

"Look, George," she said, holding up the second card.

He glanced over and grunted. "You'll want to talk to Amanda. She's got news."

She noted the grumpy tone. George didn't like "news." The more things stayed the same, the less he tended to growl. Every morning, like clockwork, he showed up at six to make the breakfasts and lunches from the cafe's menu. Every afternoon at two, like clockwork, he cleaned up after the lunch rush was over, unpacked the next day's supplies, and headed home to his wife. "I run a tight ship," he'd told her when she'd hired him four years earlier. "I like to keep things spick and span."

What George didn't like was change, since change was often messy. In her role as his boss, Holly had learned that the best way to keep him productive was to manage the messiness for him. "What's going on?" she asked.

"Better if Amanda explains." His attention was on the bacon now. "Probably not a big deal. But you never know with these things." He turned off the burner, spread a paper towel on a plate, and started transferring bacon from the pan. He gestured toward the plate. "For you for later."

"Thank you," she said.

"Gonna clean up and unpack tomorrow's stuff, then head out," he said, just as he did every day. "Two slices of yesterday's quiche still in the fridge. Took the new pie out of the oven about ten minutes ago."

"Thank you, George."

Christmas cards in hand, she stepped through the swinging doors that separated the kitchen from the cafe's spacious main room. A quick glance confirmed that all was normal for this time of day. Mid-afternoon sun filtered through the cafe's large front windows. Customers were sprinkled at four of the cafe's twelve tables, enjoying coffee, sandwiches, and scones. Warmth from the new heating system filled the room, reinforcing the cheerful coziness of the Christmas decorations — the garlands of evergreen bordering the big windows, the colorful tree ornaments — covering every available inch of the walls.

Behind the counter, her newest hire, Amanda, sat on a stool behind the cash register, her nose buried in a biology textbook. Just eighteen, a tall young woman with lanky, coltish limbs, she tended toward shyness, often hiding her face behind her long brown hair when she spoke. She was a hard worker — thoughtful and conscientious — and Holly knew she was lucky to have her. She would miss her terribly when she left for nursing school the following fall.

Holly made her way to the huge corkboard that covered a big chunk of the wall at the cafe entrance and pinned the two Christmas cards onto it, next to the dozens already up there. The corkboard, a community posting board of sorts, was open to all who wanted to announce garage sales and book clubs and events at the local community center and so much more. With Christmas fast approaching, it was now filled with news of events celebrating the season.

"Hey, Amanda," Holly said.

"Hey, boss," Amanda said, looking up from her textbook.

"George says you have something to tell me."

Amanda's expressive brown eyes immediately betrayed her nervousness. She set the textbook down and made her way from behind the counter to join Holly at the corkboard. "I ... made a management decision," she said.

Holly blinked but kept her expression neutral. She'd been encouraging Amanda to act with more confidence and take on more responsibility, but she couldn't help but be surprised that her shy young protégé had actually done exactly that.

Holly deliberately kept her tone upbeat. "A decision?"

"For the Christmas drive," Amanda said, then stopped, as if unsure how to continue.

"A great cause," Holly said encouragingly.

"You know the orchard on the outskirts of town? Northland Orchard?"

Holly had heard the name, and knew the orchard had changed hands about a year earlier, but wasn't aware of much beyond that. "Only a little bit...."

"Well, they have a new line of products — apple butters. And they're looking to promote them."

"And...."

"And they're interested in taking part in the Christmas drive."

"Oh," Holly said, beginning to relax. "That sounds great. The more local businesses we have participating, the more money we can raise."

Amanda nodded. "That's why I said yes."

"Yes to what?"

"Yes to what Mr. North — that's his name, Gabriel North — asked for."

"What did he ask for?"

Amanda rushed on. "Space."

"Space?"

"Each afternoon."

"Where?"

"Here."

Holly's back stiffened. Here? In *her* cafe? "Here?"

"A table near the door. To promote his apple butters."

It was touching how Amanda kept her eyes glued on her as she said it — nervous yet hopeful, awaiting her mentor's judgment. The request from the orchard owner was understandable, and Amanda's response to the request seemed reasonable — so what was up with her own gut-level resistance? After all, hadn't she just said it was important for more local businesses to take part in the Christmas drive? And wasn't offering up space for a table in her cafe during the holiday season actually a very easy way to demonstrate her support for her community?

How dare you let rationality get in the way of emotion, her inner voice said. *This space is yours. All yours!*

She heard her mother's voice chime in, offering the usual variations of her maddeningly carefree advice: *Calm down. Relax. Life's too short. Breathe in, breathe out. Don't sweat the small stuff.*

A table in her store — yes, perhaps it was bit of an imposition. But it would be for just a few afternoons, until the Christmas drive was over. She'd dealt with worse; she could handle this.

Decision accepted, she gave Amanda a smile. "You acted like a manager."

Amanda's posture straightened a little. "That's right."

"I'm sure it will be fine. You'll be able to work with — Mr. North, you said? — to handle table setup every day?"

"Of course."

"You're sure he's a nice person?"

"Oh, super-nice," Amanda said, "and also super-...."

She stopped before finishing the sentence. Stopped, Holly realized, before admitting that this Gabriel North was *attractive*. Which meant one of two things: Either Amanda was attracted to him for herself....

Or Amanda thought Mr. North might be a match for *Holly*.

Oh, dear.

Holly sighed. The meddling instinct ran so deep in this town. "Amanda, I hope you offered Mr. North a spot in the cafe because you want to support local businesses and a worthy charitable cause —"

"Oh, totally."

"—and not because of some other reason?"

The younger woman had the good grace to blush. But then, as if deciding to own up to everything, she shrugged and looked Holly straight in the eye. "The truth? He's good-looking. About your age. And single."

Holly slowly shook her head. Oh, to be young again, and full of enthusiasm and naiveté and hope again. "Now listen, young lady. I want to be very clear about this. In no way, shape, or form will you try to encourage or foster or nudge or concoct or play up *anything* along those lines, got it? No shenanigans, understand?"

Amanda grinned. "Got it, boss."

The door chimed and a group of customers, loaded with shopping bags full of Christmas goodies, walked in.

Amanda gestured to the counter. "I better get back to...."

"Yes, you better." Holly replied, taking Amanda by the shoulders and aiming her toward the counter. "Now scoot!"

CHAPTER 3

*A*n hour later, Holly found herself in her usual late-afternoon spot in the kitchen, kneading dough for her scones. The kitchen always got quieter — and felt emptier — after George left for the day. His pan-banging and grunts and growls were like soothing background noise; when the cacophony wasn't there, she missed it. From up front, Holly heard the familiar sounds of her mom, who usually came in to help out each afternoon, chatting happily and loudly with a customer at the counter.

The rhythms of her life — she could predict them almost to the minute. Right now, for instance, as afternoon headed toward dusk, she was almost always here, in her cafe's kitchen, making dough for tomorrow's scones. Through trial and error, she'd learned that the dough could be kept fresh and moist overnight when covered tightly with plastic wrap, so she often used the late-afternoon slowdown to make a batch or two ahead of the next morning's rush.

The dough she was making now was for a new savory scone with smoked bacon. She hadn't nailed the recipe quite yet — something else was needed — but she was getting closer. With a gentle squeeze — too much kneading took the life out of it — she took the dough from the bowl, wrapped it up, and set it in the fridge.

After washing and drying her hands, she stepped to the small desk in the corner of the kitchen where she kept her business records. Resting atop a stack of papers was a folder stuffed with notes and doodles and — most importantly — recipes of all sorts. She picked up the folder and a pen and made her way from the kitchen into the main cafe to an empty table near one of the big windows overlooking the town square. With a sigh, she settled in and opened the folder, took out the stack of papers, and started leafing through them. Each page had a recipe of something made or sold at the cafe. Her signature scones — cranberry-apple, blueberry, maple walnut, and buttermilk vanilla. The savory scones she'd started adding more recently. The delicious quiches that George made every day.

Someday soon, if she continued to apply herself, the sheaf of papers in her hands would become an actual cookbook. She even had a name picked out: *The Heartsprings Valley Cookbook: Traditions from the*

Heart. Out of the corner of her eye, she caught her reflection in the front window — a woman in her late thirties, at a table in the cafe she'd opened four years earlier with little more than grit and hope, enjoying a rare moment of relaxation in the midst of a busy day. The woman staring back at her was attractive, with shoulder-length brown hair and a nice smile, who had so much to be grateful for in her life and knew it. A wonderful family, with her mom and dad and younger brother and sister-in-law, and more recently her adorable nephew and niece. Terrific friends, with whom she could share everything. A small business she'd built from scratch. A sense of place and purpose in the town she'd grown up in.

And yet the woman sitting at the cafe window was, she acknowledged, lonely. Something — someone — was missing: a man who would become her boyfriend. A boyfriend who would become her husband. A husband with whom she would start a family. Unrealistic though that dream might be — the woman in the window was no spring chicken, not any more — the dream refused to die. The flame of hope, stubborn and unquenchable, still burned.

She blinked as she sensed movement near the counter. With the cafe momentarily quiet, her mom had ditched the register and was zooming toward her. At sixty-three, her mom was a bundle of energy, her blue eyes alive with feeling, her carefully maintained hair — auburn, with a hint of red — cut short in a bob. Today she was dressed in blue jeans and a red-white-and-green holiday sweater — she loved Christmas — with a pair of oversize gold hoop earrings and a Rudolph the red-nosed reindeer brooch for bling. She wasn't tall — she was, in fact, on the shorter side — but somehow she came across as larger-than-life.

She sat down opposite Holly and said, without preamble, "Amanda told me about the orchard guy. So I asked around."

"Is that so?" Holly murmured, deciding that now was an excellent time to pay attention to her cookbook.

"Gabriel North," her mom continued, unfazed, her tone cheerful and chatty. "Recently single. His girlfriend moved here with him, but then she dumped him and went back to New York. She didn't want to be an apple farmer. Guess that means he's no longer the apple of her eye. Ha!"

From a lifetime of experience, Holly knew better than to interfere with her mom's fact-finding missions. "Is that so?" she murmured again.

"He's a workaholic," her mom continued. "Spends day and night at that orchard of his, trying out new stuff. Apple cider and apple sauce and I don't know what else. Apparently, didn't have a clue about farming when he bought the place — not a lick of knowledge about orchards or apples — but the guys who help him say he works hard and learns quick. They're impressed with what he's doing, and you know how crusty they are, so that's saying something."

"That's great," Holly said.

"Had some kind of corporate job in New York — consultant, I think? — but got sick of it and chucked it for the simple life."

"Good for him."

"Did I mention he's single?"

Holly looked up. "Yes, Mom. Twice."

"Well, good." Then her mom went silent, choosing to gaze back at her without saying a word.

Her mom used this technique a lot. Talked up a storm, then got quiet when she wanted to make a point. Even though Holly knew the trick inside and out, even though she was no longer a child, even though she was, in fact, a grown, mature, fully inde-pendent woman, the darned technique still worked.

Holly tried to maintain a steady gaze, then gave in. "No shenanigans, Mom," she finally said. "Got it?"

"Of course, dear. Whatever you say."

"I mean it."

"I'm sure you do."

The best way out of this rabbit hole of non-verbal maternal nudging was to distract her mom with something shiny. Holly grabbed a sheet of paper and pushed it toward her. "I'm working on a new recipe.

A savory scone with bacon. It's not quite right. What do you think?"

Her mom held the recipe out at arm's length — she needed reading glasses, but preferred not to use them in public — and squinted as she read the ingredients. She was an excellent baker, with an intuitive sense of what might work and a willingness to experiment.

"Something sweet but not too sweet," her mom said. "And not a lot of it. Not sugar. Maybe maple syrup? Everyone's using maple these days." She frowned. "Try maple. It's probably not maple you want, but see what it's like. Might get you closer."

"Thank you," Holly said.

She heard a bell tinkle as the cafe's front door opened. A customer stepped in, bringing a gust of winter air with her. Her mom glanced over and stood up. "Duty calls. Think about what I said."

What you said about maple, Holly almost replied, *or what you said about Gabriel North?*

CHAPTER 4

$\mathcal{A}$s her mom launched into a lively gab-fest with the customer, Holly returned her attention to the papers in front of her. The guiding idea behind the book was to create food-and-drink pairings, with each pairing presented in the book as a two-page spread alongside biographical sidebars about the people who provided the recipes. In the four years she'd been collecting and testing recipes, she'd gathered dozens of pairings that were not only delicious and satisfying, but conveyed what her cafe — and her hometown — were all about.

The book was almost done, except for one pairing that remained glaringly incomplete: the perfect match for her signature cranberry-apple scones. She flipped to the two-page spread she'd reserved for the scone and its missing match, her brow furrowing. The empty page seemed to be taunting her, its blankness a reminder of her unfin-ished task.

Still, she couldn't beat herself up too much — the rest of the book was shaping up nicely. She turned the page to George's recipe for bacon-and-spinach quiche, a contribution as hearty and flavorful as the man himself. Somehow, it didn't seem right to call his creation a "quiche." The label, though accurate, came across as … inadequate.

She blinked when the realization struck her: She didn't have to call it that! She and George could call it anything they wanted. She crossed out "George's Bacon-and-Spinach Quiche" at the top of the page and instead wrote "George's Bacon-and-Egg Pie."

Yes, that felt better. Much better. Much more in keeping with both George and his creation. She made a mental note to run the change by him the next day.

She'd already written his sidebar biography, which read, "George Rivers, the talented, hard-working cook at Heartsprings Valley Cafe, is a Marine Corps veteran, husband, proud father, and even prouder grandfather. He and his wife Millie live in a house they built themselves on Heartsprings Ridge. Of his signature dish, he says, 'I like it because it's filling and tastes good.' To which we must add: George is being modest. His bacon-and-egg pie is complex, rich, and downright delicious. Paired with strong, dark coffee in the morning, it's the perfect start to a busy day."

She nodded to herself. Four years she'd been working on this cookbook — years that had swept by in the blink of an eye. Years spent pouring heart and soul into making the cafe a warm, inviting community space. Her eyes roved over the result of her labors: a light-filled room with big windows overlooking the snow-covered town square, filled with the pleasing aromas of fresh-baked goods, adorned with tinsel and lights and Christmas ornaments in celebration of her favorite time of the year. Up front, her mom and the customer were gabbing away merrily as her mom boxed up an order of scones.

The front door opened and a man walked in. She didn't recognize him, though as the thought entered her head, she sensed that wasn't quite right. She'd seen him before — but where? He was tall, six feet at least, and carried himself like an athlete, with dark brown hair and a handsome face. He was dressed in jeans and work boots and a mackinaw jacket over a blue-and-red flannel shirt. Maybe in his late thirties? Reflexively, she searched for the third finger of his left hand, frowning when she found it hidden from her line of sight.

Her jaw clenched when she realized what she was doing. Why would it matter to her whether the man happened to be married or not?

At the counter, her mom turned to the stranger. "Good afternoon! How can I help you?"

The man said, in a confident voice, "I was hoping to speak with Ms. Snow, the owner."

At the table, Holly's back straightened with surprise.

"Oh," her mom said, curiosity in her tone, her eyes darting Holly's way. "And you are?"

"My name's Gabe North. I run Northland Orchard, right outside of town."

Her mom's face lit up. "You're the orchard guy!"

Gabe blinked, taken aback. "I guess so?"

"Welcome to the Heartsprings Valley Cafe. Amanda told me all about you."

Holly's stomach clenched as she realized her mom could easily steer the conversation in a dangerous direction — and that simply wouldn't do. She got to her feet, ran her hand through her hair, licked her lips, and glanced at her reflection in the window, suddenly wishing she'd picked a different blouse that morning. Squaring her shoulders, she stepped toward the counter.

"Holly," her mom said, "a gentleman to see you."

The gentleman — Gabe — turned her way. When he saw her, his face and body went still. Like he was surprised. And by the way his brown eyes lit up — they were nice brown eyes, she saw now, warm and expressive — the surprise seemed of the agreeable sort.

Before those initial impressions even flashed by, she found herself saying, in a voice that relieved her with its steadiness, "Mr. North? I'm Holly Snow." Her hand, moving on its own volition, reached out to take his.

He unfroze. "Ms. Snow? Pleased to meet you." Was there a hint of nervousness in his voice now? He stepped forward — he was a good inch or two taller than six feet, she realized, and his shoulders looked broad and strong — and took her hand in his.

She nearly gasped aloud as a jolt raced through her. Not an electric shock, exactly, but still … something indefinable, something real.

"Pleased to meet you, too," she said automatically, her brain falling back onto the well-worn response. His hand was warm, with a hint of roughness from his work at the orchard. "And please, no 'Ms. Snow.' Call me Holly."

His grin widened, even as his hand lingered. "Gabe. Call me Gabe."

She became aware their handshake was going on longer than might be considered typical. With reluctance, she withdrew and took a small step back. "How can I help you, Gabe?"

"Well," he said, his brown eyes still taking her in, "I wanted to meet you. I was here earlier today and spoke with Amanda, and she was really helpful, but she wasn't the owner, so I wanted to make sure that what she and I discussed is okay." He paused, then said, "With you, I mean."

Holly nodded. "Amanda told me she met you,

and agreed to let you set up a table in the cafe for the Christmas charity drive."

"That's right," he said.

"To market your orchard's new products."

"That's right."

"You're more than welcome. It's no problem at all. The more local businesses taking part in the Christmas drive, the better."

"Great," he said, exhaling. "Really glad to hear that. I know it's an imposition. I appreciate the opportunity."

She liked that he understood and acknowledged that. She surprised herself by saying, "If you don't mind my asking: If you knew it would be an imposition, why did you ask?"

He paused, clearly not expecting the question, then said, "I guess ... because you never really know. Because if you don't ask, you never get to yes."

"Spoken like a true entrepreneur."

He grinned. "I bet you and I could swap tales about what it takes to start and run a small business."

"I bet we could," she said, smiling back. "So ... what would you have done if I'd said no?"

His eyes roved over the cafe. "I would have been disappointed. What you have here is beautiful — warm, inviting, smells great. The perfect place to introduce the new line of Northland Orchard apple butters."

"The bookstore," she said. "I would have gone to the bookstore."

"Good to know," he replied with a gleam in his eye.

"Just bring a fresh apple pie with you — the owner loves apple pie — and she'll be your friend for life."

He laughed.

At that moment, she heard the sound of a throat being cleared. She'd forgotten — her mom was standing right there!

"Gabe," she said hurriedly, "let me introduce you to my mother, Beverly Snow."

He turned and reached out his hand. "Mrs. Snow, a pleasure to meet you."

"Bev — call me Bev," her mom said, grabbing Gabe's hand and giving it a vigorous shake. "You're so right about not being afraid to ask for what you want, Gabriel. Do you like Gabe or Gabriel?"

"Either's fine," Gabe said as he extricated his hand.

"Mom helps out in the afternoons," Holly said.

"Since you and I will be hanging out the next few days," her mom said, "I'll call you Gabriel. I like that name. I like how it sounds when I say it — Gay-Bree-El. I want to hear all about the orchard business. I don't know a thing about apples except how to eat 'em and bake 'em. Did Amanda say something about apple butter?"

He stared at her for a few seconds, trying to absorb everything she'd just thrown at him, then said, "That's right. A new line of apple butters." He reached into his jacket pocket, pulled out a small jar, and set it on the counter. "Here's a sample. I'll bring more tomorrow."

Her mom picked up the jar and held it at arm's length so she could read the label. "Northland Orchard Sweet Apple Butter," she said out loud.

Holly stepped closer, curious. "Can I see?"

Her mom handed her the jar. Holly allowed herself to feel it, weigh it, and adjust her hand to its contours, her thoughts moving into business and marketing mode. The apple butter was caramel-colored, and the label a deep blue-gray, with bright white lettering in an antique script that would be easily readable on a retail shelf.

"The label is lovely," Holly said. "Did you design it yourself?"

"A buddy in New York who works in advertising."

"Do you have other kinds of apple butters?"

He nodded. "We have three different apples at the orchard — Baldwin, McIntosh, and Blushing Golden — and a butter for each. And we just introduced a fourth butter — a blend."

Her mom chimed in. "What time are you showing up tomorrow? I can be here to help."

"Early afternoon okay?" he asked, glancing between her mom and Holly.

"Perfect," her mom replied.

Holly said, "Do you need a folding table?"

"No, I'll bring everything I need."

"Great," Holly said. "We'll clear a space near the door."

With tomorrow's logistics handled, she found herself pausing, unsure how to proceed. He didn't seem to be in a hurry — if anything, his attention seemed as glued on her as hers was on him. On his right cheek, she noticed stubble from a spot he'd missed while shaving that morning. He really was quite handsome, what with that thick head of dark brown hair, those big brown eyes, that strong jaw....

As the pause grew awkward, Holly felt her cheeks blush. "Sorry, what did you say?"

"Nothing," he said, blinking suddenly. "I mean, I didn't say anything." He swallowed and loosened his shoulders. "I guess I should be going. I'm glad I swung by."

"And asked," her mom added.

He shot her an appreciative glance. "Absolutely. Very glad I asked."

"We're glad you asked, too. Isn't that right, Holly?"

"Of course," Holly said.

Gabe grinned. "Holly, Bev, pleased to meet you both. See you tomorrow."

With a smile, he turned and left.

The two women watched him fade into the darkness outside.

Holly turned to her mom, a warning look on her face.

Her mom grinned right back, unabashed. "Did you notice? Just like I said. No ring."

"*Mom….*"

Her mom threw up her hands in protest. "Just sayin'…."

"There's never any 'just saying' when it comes to you."

"Oh, Holly, you worry too much." She grabbed the sample jar from Holly's hand and twisted it open. "Shall we?" She grabbed a spoon from the counter and scooped out a small dollop. Delicately, she brought the spoon to her mouth and closed her eyes.

For several long seconds, her mom didn't say anything — just stood there like a statue.

Again, despite knowing how utterly predictable it was to fall into her mom's silence trap, Holly couldn't help herself. "Well?"

Her mom opened her eyes and held out the spoon and jar. "Try some for yourself."

Holly took the jar, scooped out a bit, and leaned in for a taste. Despite her years in the kitchen, she wasn't familiar with apple butter. The texture — smooth and almost jam-like — was a bit of a surprise, as was the richness, the depth of flavor.

"I like it," Holly said.

"I like it, too."

"It's actually quite delicious."

"Rather dreamy, in fact."

"We're talking about the apple butter, right?"

"What else could we be talking about?"

"What I said, Mom? I mean it."

"Of course you do," her mom replied, then glanced at her watch. "Oh, will you look at the time." She reached under the counter and grabbed her purse and winter coat. "Your father is probably rooting around the refrigerator right now, scrounging for scraps. I better get home before he eats all the left-overs." She shrugged into her coat, then bustled around the counter and gave Holly a peck on the cheek. "See you tomorrow, dear. You and Gay-Bree-El."

"Mom…."

"Goodnight, dear!" Before Holly could say another word, her mom scooted out the door and vanished into the night.

CHAPTER 5

*T*he following morning, as Holly stared blankly at the clothes hanging in her closet and tried to settle on what to wear, the thought wouldn't go away: Her mom could be so *silly* sometimes. The way some people acted when it came to romance — it just wasn't realistic. The notion that two busy grownups could be maneuvered into instant attraction was pure nonsense. She'd have to keep an eye out for any such attempts by her mom or Amanda. Especially her mom, whose enthusiasm for new ideas sometimes went a bit overboard.

She frowned as she returned to the task at hand. Her closet wasn't cooperating with her. Usually it offered up options easily, but this morning, for whatever reason, none of her go-to choices was calling her name. She pulled out a pink silk blouse, held it up in front of her, and turned to examine herself in the full-length mirror on the wall next to the closet door. No, too dressy. She'd already picked her dark black slacks — no jeans today — so whatever she wore with them would need to match.

She returned the blouse to the rack and took out a light-blue button-down collared shirt. This one felt more like spring than winter. On the flip side, it fit well and worked with the slacks, so....

She nodded. Yes, this was the one.

A glance at the watch on her left wrist told her she was running late. Well, not late — nineteen minutes after five in the morning was super-early for most people — but she was definitely behind schedule. Usually at this moment in her day, she was already on her way to the cafe, not standing in her bedroom in front of the mirror, torn with indecision about her clothing choices.

Time to get your you-know-what in gear. With a sigh, she buttoned herself into the shirt, checked her makeup in the mirror — she'd also spent more time than normal on her blush and mascara and lip gloss — and made her way downstairs. A minute later, suitably bundled up, she headed into the darkness for the short walk to her cafe.

She'd always enjoyed these moments of quiet, with most of her neighbors still slumbering in their beds, the streets empty of cars, the sidewalks hers alone. The inky blackness of the night sky, punctuated by the twinkling of distant stars, held no hint yet of the approaching dawn. The crisp morning air, still and seemingly at peace, was the polar opposite of what she'd encountered the morning before, when blustery winds had effortlessly penetrated her thick winter coat. Christmas decorations adorned most of the homes she passed, their cheerful lights reflected in the snow already on the ground.

As she approached the town square, a smile found its way to her lips. How lucky she was to live in Heartsprings Valley. How fortunate to grow up here. She knew every inch of the snowman-filled town square, and every small business along its four sides. On an impulse, instead of walking directly across the square to her cafe, she turned left and strolled past the shops lining the square.

At the local chocolate shop run by her friend Abby, she paused in front of the display window, leaning in to admire the holiday-themed gingerbread house that held a place of honor amidst Abby's usual arrangement of tempting chocolate treats. Created by the town's librarian, Becca Shepherd, the gingerbread house was an homage to the town's Heartsprings Valley Inn, complete with dramatic Queen Anne gables and a large wraparound porch. Becca's skill as a gingerbread artist came through in the details: the light snow dusting the roof, the string of holiday garlands lining the porch, and even the Christmas tree visible inside through the windows.

Her stomach rumbled as she imagined biting into

one of Abby's delicious handmade chocolate treats. Yes, she'd have to pop in for a visit and get herself a much-needed fix — perhaps a truffle or two or three, or maybe a caramel nougat, or something in dark chocolate, or...?

Control thyself, she admonished herself — very half-heartedly — before continuing down the block to Cane Hardware, owned and operated by her friend Ted. The store's big display window was always good for a healthy dose of holiday happiness, and this year's panorama was, in Holly's humble opinion, the store's best yet. Ted's fiancée Peggy and daughter Clara had spent months planning every inch of it, and the results were terrific — a true smorgasbord of cherished Christmas traditions. On a track running the length of the display was a model electric train. And not just any train, but the North Pole Express, loaded with toys and goodies, packed with elves and kids, and decorated in tiny strings of festive red-and-green lights. Even now, in the pre-dawn darkness, it was chugging merrily away.

As her eyes followed the train, she took note of the other traditions packed into the display: a beautiful Christmas tree adorned with all manner of ornaments; a big stack of brightly wrapped presents; a snowy marshmallow field with an army of marshmallow snowmen and snowwomen and snowkids, all with big smiles on their faces; and up above, hanging from nearly invisible string, Santa and his sleigh, pulled by his crew of enthusiastic reindeer. Somehow, Clara and Peggy had found a way — perhaps with a small battery? — to make Rudolph's red nose glow. And across the bottom of the display, she spied a touch she hadn't noticed before, a message written in the marshmallow snow using baby pine cones: *Joy to the World.*

Reluctantly, she tore her gaze from the window and continuing strolling past the other shops, her pace picking up as she neared her destination. She and the other store owners were such a tight group, all of them working together to contribute to the town's vibrant spirit. Like with the Christmas drive. She made a mental note to call the participating businesses that afternoon to see how much closer they were getting to their fundraising goal. Support for veterans and their families was so important. The more they could raise, the better.

Up ahead, she saw the handpainted wooden sign extending from the space that, for the past four years, had been her pride and joy: Heartsprings Valley Cafe. Her dad had built the sign in his garage workshop using reclaimed cedar. She'd lightly stained the wood a soft grey, then designed and painted the lettering herself — "Heartsprings Valley" in cheerful bright red and "Cafe" in creamy white. Even at night, the letters were easy to read against the grey background. A fringe of evergreen, painted in the corners, completed the look. Though she hadn't consciously planned to make the sign feel like Christmas, there was no denying she'd done just that.

At the cafe's front door, she slipped the key into the lock and stepped inside. As always, she stood silently in the darkness for a few long seconds, letting the quiet linger, appreciating all that she had to be grateful for, allowing herself one last moment of peace before things got busy. She imagined she could hear the cafe whispering its welcome, eager for the new day to begin. She made her way behind the counter and through the swinging doors into the kitchen, where she turned on the lights. She stepped to her small desk in the back and, after hanging up her coat, flipped open the laptop on the desk. With a quick glance at the clock on the opposite wall — she was off to a later start than usual, so she'd have to speed through her morning routine to catch up — she sat down and attacked the stack of mail that she'd let pile up the past few days. Most were the usual bills and bank statements and the like, but one piece of mail caught her eye: a postcard from Northland Orchard. The front showed a photo of a row of apple trees dusted with fresh snowfall — probably snapped a few weeks earlier, after the season's first snow. "Join us for an old-fashioned Wassail!" the postcard announced.

Wassail? Her brow furrowed as she tried to recall exactly what that meant. Did it have something to do with apples? She flipped over the postcard and read:

"Northland Orchard invites you to an old-fashioned evening of wassailing with songs, ciders, sleigh rides, and more." The event was taking place in three nights. She set the postcard at the top of her paper stack. She'd have to ask Gabe about it when he showed up later.

From up front, she heard the sound of the front door opening, and a few seconds later, George stepped in.

"Morning, boss," he said as he always did.

"Morning, George."

He hung up his coat, took off his hat and gloves, and glanced at the pristine prep station. "Late start?"

She nodded, then closed the laptop and stood up. "Just a bit."

His eyes landed on her blue collared shirt and dark slacks. "Why so dressed up?"

"Oh, no reason," she replied, aware of how self-conscious the question made her. "Just felt like it, I guess."

He stared at her for a second, then shrugged and got to work.

She followed his example and slipped on her apron. Very quickly, the morning became a steady rush of familiar tasks. There were scones and muffins to bake, pots of coffee to brew, juices and yogurts to take out of the fridge and move up front, sugar and cream containers to fill, new coffee cups and coffee lids to set out, plates and glasses to take out of the dishwashers, and so much more. Shortly before seven, she turned on the lights in the front room, set the sound system to the local radio station's month-long Christmas music marathon, flipped the sign on the door to "Open," and unlocked the front door.

A few minutes later, when the first customer arrived, the day got under way.

CHAPTER 6

*T*he first hint that the presence of a certain orchard owner might prove distracting to her team became apparent that afternoon, when Holly returned from her daily power walk. A folding table had been set up near the door while she was out.

From her spot at the cash register, Amanda leaned forward and said, with barely suppressed excitement, "He went to his truck to get the rest of his stuff."

"I see," Holly replied.

"Is the table positioned okay?"

"Yes, it's fine," Holly said. "Does Mr. North — Gabe — need a tablecloth?"

"He said he has everything covered."

Holly glanced again at the counter. Something else besides her protégé's nervous excitement was different — but what? Then it hit her: The biology textbook wasn't there.

"No studying today?"

"Oh," Amanda said. "Maybe later. When Gabe arrived, I was helping him, so…."

Holly was about to dispense some advice about the importance of academic preparation when her eye caught movement on the sidewalk outside the cafe. Gabe was approaching, a big box in his arms. And next to him, gabbing away merrily, was —

Her mom?

Holly's eyes narrowed. What was Mom doing here so early? Usually she didn't arrive for her afternoon shift for another hour, sometimes later. Certainly she never showed up *this* early. What was she up to?

Her mom pulled open the cafe door for Gabe. "You got it, dear?" she said to him as he moved past her and carefully set the box on the folding table near the door.

"Yep," Gabe said. "Thanks."

Holly's stomach clenched. Oh, my — her mom had called him *dear*.

The shenanigans specialist turned to Holly and beamed. "You should see what Gabriel brought — it looks so yummy!"

"I'm sure it is," Holly said as she watched her mom eagerly unload the box.

Gabe shrugged out of his coat, set it on the chair

behind the table, and turned toward her. "Afternoon, Holly." He was dressed much like yesterday — jeans and work boots — although his crisp light-blue collared shirt was a step up from the previous day's flannel.

"Good afternoon, Gabe."

"Thanks again for letting me do this." His gaze caused an involuntary flutter in her chest.

"Oh, not a problem at all."

He glanced at his helper, who was now busily unloading the box. "Bev, I appreciate it, but really, there's no need."

"Nonsense," her mom said firmly. "Happy to help."

Curious about what Gabe had brought and eager to shift attention to a safe topic, Holly stepped closer for a look. Jars of apple butter were getting piled on the table — four different kinds, going by the labels. She picked up a jar with a burgundy-red label and "Northland Orchard's Cinnamon Apple Butter" in crisp white type.

"I think you said you have a butter for each type of apple?" she asked.

He nodded. "Each with a different flavor profile. This one — Baldwin — is from the oldest trees on the farm. The apple has a spicy, sweet-tart flavor, which we've tried to capture in the butter and complement with the cinnamon."

Holly found herself being drawn in, her mind

starting to think of possible uses. "You know," she said, "I'd like to give these a try and see how we might be able to use them here."

He glanced toward the counter display of tempting scones and muffins. "You mean, with these?"

"Yes."

He stepped closer and bent down to examine the various baked goods. "You make these here?"

"In the back, every day."

"I see cranberry-apple, blueberry, maple.... Is that bacon?"

"Yes, a smoked bacon scone I'm trying out."

"A born experimenter?"

She smiled. "Can't help myself."

He stood up and turned toward her. "Your experiments smell delicious."

"Thank you." She held his gaze for a long second, her insides warmed by his words and attention, until she realized that movement around them had ceased. She glanced over and found her mom and Amanda watching them. Her mom had a small smile on her face and Amanda was wide-eyed with curiosity.

Oh, dear.

Holly coughed. "Mom, why don't we step back and give Gabe room to set up?"

Her mom turned to Gabe and said, very brightly, "Let's open a sample jar for each apple butter at the front of the table. I'm sure folks would love to try them out. We can stack the jars in pyramids behind them."

"Sounds good," Gabe said, shooting Holly a smile before turning his attention to the table. "I'll get the tablecloth." Together, he and her mom quickly got the table set up. After clearing off the jars of apple butter, Gabe grabbed a vibrant red tablecloth — the perfect color for Christmas — and draped it over the table. Her mom picked up the apple butters and started arranging them into four pyramids, while Gabe took kid-size boxes of apple juice in colorful containers from the box, followed by several jugs of apple cider.

Holly watched them as they worked, marveling at how effortless they made it seem. The way they moved and divvied up the tasks — it was like they'd known each other forever, their actions smoothly choreographed, no communication required. Her mom had always known instinctively how to sync up with others. If only Holly could make such a claim herself. For herself, alas, moments of awkwardness were an inescapable part of living.

Like right now, she realized. She was feeling awkward because she was just standing here, while they did all the work.

"Let me get sample spoons for the butters," she said. Quickly, she escaped into the kitchen, where George was in the middle of his afternoon cleanup.

Sponge in hand, he threw her a frown, clearly unsettled by the hubbub up front.

"I think we have a box of small sample spoons somewhere," Holly said.

"Pantry, bottom shelf, green box."

"Thank you." She made her way to the pantry, bent down, and rooted through the green box until she found what she wanted. The spoons were in a small red box of their own. When she opened the lid, she could almost hear the spoons say, "Finally! We can't wait to get busy."

She stood up, stretched her back, then stepped back into the kitchen, where George was giving the sink a very aggressive scrubbing.

"They're almost done setting up out there," she said. "Things will settle down soon."

He gave her the grouch-eye but didn't say anything.

"It'll be like he isn't even there."

He snorted and scrubbed even harder.

"What?" she said, aware, even as the question left her mouth, that she was coming across as defensive.

"I didn't say anything," George said.

"No, but you want to. I can tell. Come on, help me out."

He stopped his scrubbing and aimed his eyes at her. "Your shirt. And your slacks."

Her cheeks flushed as the implication of his

words sunk in. "What about them?" she asked, though she knew exactly what he meant.

"And his shirt," he said, ignoring her question and pressing his point.

She blinked. "What about his shirt?"

He gave her a long, mournful look. With a sigh, he put the sponge down and rinsed his hands under the faucet. "Maybe you're right," he finally said as he turned off the water and dried his hands. "Maybe he'll come and go and everything will go back to the way it used to be."

"That's right," she said, though the words sounded hollow as she said them.

He looked at her for a second or two, his gaze conveying decades of life experience. Finally, like a balloon releasing pressure to avoid bursting, he exhaled. "Okay, boss. Heading out. Wife's waiting. New pie on the counter. See you in the morning."

CHAPTER 7

*A*n hour later, as the afternoon sun cast ever-lengthening shadows across the kitchen counter, Holly was half-in, half-out of autopilot mode.

On the half-in side: Her hands, operating on muscle memory alone, were busy making dough.

On the half-out side: The thought rattling through her head simply wouldn't go away. Much as she didn't want to admit it, she had to accept that George was right to be concerned. Gabe's presence was proving a distraction.

But not in the way she'd expected. After the initial flurry of setup activities, the cafe's front room had settled down nicely. Gabe was at his table, chatting with curious customers and dispensing samples of apple butter and cider. Her mom was behind the counter, where a steady stream of customers was keeping her busy.

No, the distraction was within herself. If today were a normal day, right now she'd be focusing on her usual list of late-afternoon chores — which wouldn't get done by themselves — rather than the worrying question that kept raising its hand, begging for attention, like a smart-alecky kid in class. Namely: What about her treasured late-afternoon ritual, where she brought her cookbook to the front of the cafe and sat down at the table near the window and worked on her book? How could she go out there and focus on her project with Gabe sitting just ten feet away?

Another voice pushed back: What was she worrying about? Surely she could explain to Gabe what she was doing and why, and surely he'd understand and leave her in peace. He seemed like a reasonable, considerate individual. He'd understand.

She sighed with frustration. *Girl, you just need to take a chill pill.* A glance at the dough revealed that she'd pummeled it enough, perhaps too much. "Sorry," she said out loud, then took it out of the bowl, set it on the counter, and sliced it into triangles. After arranging the pieces on a baking pan, she wrapped the pan carefully in plastic wrap and set it in the fridge to chill.

She stretched her back, her muscles aching from the tension she'd been carrying. She'd delayed long enough. The cafe was hers, the cookbook was her project, and she had every right to work on her book where and when she pleased.

She rinsed and dried her hands, then walked to her desk, where the book folder was waiting for her, silently urging her to open it. She picked it up, ran her tongue over her lips and, with a nervous flutter, made her way through the swinging doors.

Both Gabe and her mom were busy with customers — perfect. She made a beeline for her favorite table, sat down, and eagerly opened the folder, ready to dive in. But as she stared at the pages with willful determination, she realized the recipes weren't beckoning. The distraction she'd experienced in the kitchen was proving an even tougher nut to crack out here. Despite her fervent desire to lose herself in her good book, she was uncomfortably aware that the customer chatting with Gabe was now saying goodbye and heading out. The sound of the door opening and the gust of cold air from outside confirmed that the customer was no longer there. Which meant she had no earthly need for visual confirmation. No, that simple action wasn't needed at all.

But of course her head and eyes betrayed her. Her head moved and her eyes followed. Almost like they couldn't help but look in the direction of a certain orchard owner. Almost like they wanted to see —

Gabe looking at her.

Which he was.

And he'd noticed her noticing!

"Hey, Holly," he said.

"Hey," she said, her cheeks flushing.

He gestured to the folder in front of her. "What are you working on?"

She opened her mouth, then closed it. She hadn't anticipated him being interested in the cookbook. Why hadn't she considered that possibility? What was wrong with her?

"This? Oh, it's...."

He waited for her to finish her sentence, his gaze open and curious.

"It's a cookbook," she finally said.

"That's interesting," he said, looking impressed. "What kind of cookbook?"

"Recipes that represent the spirit of Heartsprings Valley."

"Can I take a look?" he asked, like he meant it. "If you don't mind, that is."

"Of course," she said, her pulse ratcheting up.

He rose, strode to her table, grabbed a chair, set it next to hers, and sat down. All in a few seconds. Boy, when Mr. North moved, he didn't waste time. The room became a bit warmer than usual, the air a bit more still. It was like time was slowing, ever so slightly, to allow her to take in the tiny little details of this moment. Like his blue collared shirt — a color that looked good on him, complementing his brown hair and eyes. She caught a hint of aftershave — not much, just a trace. On one of his wrists, she noticed his watch, one of those solid, indestructible metal numbers that men seemed to regard as essential to the continued survival of the species. No ring on either hand, as her mom had already pointed out.

He leaned forward, his shoulders nearly touching hers. Mere inches away. Not that she minded. Far from that, actually. Talk about distracting!

"So," she said, a bit more loudly than she'd intended. "How's the table going so far?"

"Terrific." He was looking right at her, his attention completely on her. "Thanks again for letting me set up here. Already met a bunch of neighbors and had some great conversations."

"Glad to hear," she said, willing herself to maintain eye contact despite her nervousness.

He pointed to the folder in front of her. "Tell me about the cookbook."

She swallowed. For reasons she didn't have time to sort through right now, his response to the cookbook was suddenly very important. She bit back a nervous smile, took a deep breath, and launched into her standard description. "When I started the cafe four years ago, I wanted an opportunity to showcase the recipes we offer, and I realized a cookbook would be a great way to do that. So I started writing down recipes and including them in this folder."

"A great idea and a great project," he said, his

gaze shifting from the pages back to her. "Totally in line with what you do here at the cafe."

"Absolutely," she said, warming to the subject. "Gradually, as the book began to take shape, I realized the opportunity was even bigger. The recipes were about more than just the cafe — they had stories to tell, stories that spoke to what Heartsprings Valley is all about. So the book has grown to reflect that. It's still very much a cookbook, but it's also about the folks who live here. Folks I grew up with. Folks I've known my entire life. Each of the recipe pairings —"

"Pairings?" he asked, eyebrows rising.

"Let me show you." She flipped through the pages and landed on a two-page spread. "For example, this pairing combines a scone and a hot cocoa. Both are great recipes in their own right, but together they're even stronger. The scone is the cafe's hazelnut-cherry scone. The cocoa is Auntie Minerva's special recipe for hot cocoa."

"Auntie Minerva? I don't think I've met her."

"Auntie Minerva is Minerva Heartsprings, the last descendant of our town's founding family. She passed a few years back, at the age of 102. I knew her growing up. She told me and the other kids wonderful stories about the old days."

His eyes scanned the recipes for the scone and the hot cocoa, then looked back at her, eyes gleaming. "Just so you know, you're making me hungry. Very hungry. My mouth is watering."

She warmed to his words. "Along with the recipes, the book includes brief snapshots of the folks who came up with the recipes."

"Do you mind if I…?" he asked, indicating that he wanted to flip through more pages.

"Please do."

Carefully, he began moving from pairing to pairing. "These look great," he said. "I really like how you're doing this."

"Thank you."

"And I really like *why* you're doing this."

She felt an unexpected surge of emotion at his words — surprise and also gratitude.

"I mean," he said, "this works on so many levels. From a business perspective, of course, it makes total sense."

"Agreed," she said.

"Even more importantly, it represents you. And this town, and your connection to it."

"That's my hope, yes."

"I could learn a thing or two from this. And from you."

"From me?" she said, surprised.

"You've figured out how to run a small business. You've been doing it for — four years?" When she nodded, he continued. "Clearly, a big part of your success is how you've built and maintained strong connections with the local community."

She nodded. "The cafe wouldn't exist without the love and support of my friends and neighbors."

"See? The way you put it is perfect."

"Compared with how you put it?"

He shrugged. "Sometimes I get caught up in jargon. I went to business school and worked as a consultant, which meant learning and regurgitating way too many acronyms and way too much lingo. And while those experiences were great — I learned a lot that's come in handy with the orchard — sometimes I have trouble letting go of the technical terms and keeping it real."

"Keeping it real?"

"What I mean," he said, warming to his topic, "is that a business is about more than balance sheets and inventory controls and depreciation schedules and the like. Don't get me wrong — that stuff is important, too. But a great business is, at its heart, about service. If you're running your business the right way, then you're making your customers happy and contributing to your community."

He meant what he said — she saw that clear as day. His passion couldn't be more sincere.

"That's why you're here in Heartsprings Valley, isn't it?" she said. "You want something real."

He went still, his eyes locked on hers. "That's right. Something tangible. Something I can dive into."

She pointed to the apple butters on the table. "Something you can grow. And taste."

He grinned. "You sure we didn't know each other in a past life?"

She smiled back. "A lot of small-business owners feel the same. What we do means everything to us."

"Just so you know," he said, his grin widening, "usually, when I'm getting to know someone, I don't jump right away into deep and meaningful. I usually open with light and inconsequential."

"Ah, yes," she said. "Much safer."

"Way safer."

"Something like the weather?"

"Always a good starter."

"Pretty cold one today, isn't it?"

"Getting even colder tonight, I hear."

They grinned at each other, allowing the moment to linger. He really was fun to talk with — smart, too. And he had a way of making her feel so comfortable.

She was about to say more when she sensed a flurry of movement out of the corner of her eye.

Uh oh.

Her stomach clenched at the sight of her mom bustling toward them.

"Gay-Bree-El," her mom said, waving a postcard in her hand. "What in the world is *this*?"

CHAPTER 8

*H*olly willed her expression to remain neutral, even as she tensed in preparation for whatever ploy her mom had up her sleeve. She glanced toward the counter, searching in vain for a customer she could ask her mom to go help. But no. For the moment, at least, the cafe was quiet.

Her mom, with an inquisitive air, set the postcard on the table in front of Gabe. "Tell me more."

Holly glanced down. It was the postcard she'd found earlier in the stack of mail, for the Wassail event at Gabe's orchard.

"Ah," Gabe said. "The Wassail. Hopefully, the start of a new holiday tradition at Northland Orchard." He gestured toward an empty chair. "Take a seat. Happy to tell you all about it."

"Thank you," her mom said as she settled in.

"When I read this, I thought, 'A Wassail? What the heck is that?'"

Gabe smiled. "It's an old English tradition that goes back centuries. Basically, folks get together to enjoy a cider-based drink called 'wassail' and sing to the apple trees to encourage them to produce lots of apples in the coming year."

"You sing?" her mom asked. "To the trees? To cheer them up? To make them happier?"

"That's the idea."

"Well, I like it," she said, nodding vigorously. "And it makes perfect sense. You know I talk to my flowers all the time."

Gabe grinned. "You're a plant whisperer?"

Her mom laughed. "Not a whisperer — I'm too high-volume for that — but yes, I think my plants enjoy hearing what's going on." She shot a glance at Holly. "Though my daughter doesn't think that's realistic."

"I never said that, Mom," Holly protested.

"Oh, but you did," her mom said, then turned to Gabe. "She was sixteen. Very sure of herself. I can still hear her exact words. 'Plants don't have *ears*, Mom. They can't *hear*.'"

Holly laughed. "Did I really say that?"

"You did."

"Okay, I'll admit, that does sound like me." She glanced toward Gabe and shrugged. "That's what being sixteen was about, at least for me. Lots of firm convictions."

Gabe chuckled. "I've been reading a lot in the past year about farming and productivity and growing techniques. There are some interesting studies about the beneficial impacts of music, speech, and other sounds on plant growth."

Her mom beamed. "See? I knew it."

"So," Holly said, "is that why you're doing a Wassail? To increase orchard productivity?"

"No. I mean, if it turns out the trees produce more apples because they love Christmas carols, then I'll serenade them with 'Jingle Bells' all year long. But that's not the reason."

"So what is the reason?" her mom said.

He shrugged. "My family's always known, in a general way, that our ancestors came from England, but we never knew specifics. So a few years back, when my dad retired, he embarked on a big genealogy project to discover our family's history. He and Mom got really into it — started having a lot of fun — so two summers ago, they flew to England and spent several weeks doing research on the ground, poking around libraries and church archives and records offices."

"Oh, I'd love to do that," her mom breathed.

"What they discovered is that on my dad's side, we're descended from a long line of farmers from Gloucestershire in the south of England. And it turns out that, for several decades in the mid-1800s, our ancestors hosted Wassails on their farms — big events with all of their neighbors."

"So you're reviving an old family tradition," her mom said.

"That's right."

Her mom picked up the postcard and read it again. "And it takes place in two nights. At your orchard."

"In the early evening. Ciders and caroling and more."

"You inviting a lot of folks?"

"With a big assist from Mayor Winters. He's been great — really supportive and helpful. I'm new here and don't know many people yet. He's been doing everything he can to spread the word."

Holly nodded. "That's Bert Winters in a nutshell — full of energy."

"And ideas," Gabe added. "When he told me about the annual Christmas charity drive, I knew right away that I wanted to help."

"So the Wassail event is part of the charity drive?"

"Yep, absolutely."

"That's great. Every little bit will help us reach our fundraising goal."

"Speaking of…. Are we going to hit the target?"

Probably not, she almost admitted. Earlier that afternoon, she'd checked in with the other local merchants. The totals so far, while good, were pointing to a near-miss. "We'll see."

Her mom said, "Holly and I will be happy to help out."

Holly blinked as her mom's words sank in. *What?*

Before Holly could open her mouth to protest, Gabe held up his hand. "Bev, I appreciate the offer — really I do." He glanced toward Holly. "But I'm sure you have a ton of stuff going on here. How about this: I'd be honored if you both could attend — as guests."

"Of course," her mom said. "We'll be there. Right, dear?"

Two pairs of eyes swung toward her. Holly put a smile on her face. "Yes, of course. Count us in."

"That's great," he said with a grin. "I look forward to having you there as invited guests." He glanced at his watch and gave a start. "Oops, running late. Errands to get done." He stood up. "Thank you both again for everything today — really appreciate it."

"Glad we could help," Holly said.

"See you tomorrow?" he asked, his eyes aimed right at her.

"See you tomorrow."

She watched while he shrugged into his coat and headed out.

As the door closed behind him, Holly whirled on her mom. "What did I say about shenanigans?"

"I don't know what you mean, dear," her mom said, choosing that moment to examine her fingernails.

"*Mom….*"

Her mom looked back up, almost defiantly. "I was just being neighborly. What's wrong with being neighborly? And what about the charity drive? Don't you want to help the charity drive?"

"Mom…."

The cafe doorbell tinkled as a customer stepped in. Her mom jumped up. "Gotta go."

"We're not done talking about this."

"What is this 'this' about which we are talking?" her mom said as she bustled away.

"The 'this' about which we are —" Holly said, then stopped when it became clear that her mom was ignoring her.

She sighed with frustration. If she was being honest with herself, the knot in her stomach at that moment was her own fault, not her mom's. Had she been paying closer attention, she would have anticipated her mom's maneuver and understood that, when her mom asked Gabe about his Wassail event, her question was merely a prelude, a ruse, a blatant ploy to get Holly and Gabe to spend more time together. She knew her mom inside and out — she should have seen it coming. So why hadn't she?

Because you like your mom's plan, her inner voice whispered.

Her stomach clenched tighter. *And you were secretly cheering her on.*

Argh. She stood up. She didn't have time for this unrealistic nonsense. She had tasks to tackle. A cafe to run. She gathered up the recipe folder and marched back to the kitchen.

The "this" about which she was talking — her silly daydreaming about Gabe — was exactly that. Unrealistic nonsense!

CHAPTER 9

*M*uch to Holly's chagrin, the distraction caused by her less-than-realistic daydreaming show no signs of dissipating the following day. Once again, her early-morning routine was slowed by spending too much time agonizing over makeup and what to wear. Even after arriving at the cafe (in black slacks and a crisp white button-down blouse) and settling into her normal rush of activity, she found herself perking up every time she heard the cafe door open, her rebellious mind wondering if Gabe had arrived.

As morning passed into early afternoon and the lunch rush slowed with no Gabe in sight, Holly realized she was being silly. After all, he'd asked for space to set up and man the table each *afternoon*, not each morning *and* afternoon. Running an orchard took a lot of work — no doubt he was busy. Doing what, exactly, she had no idea — orchards were not her specialty — but it was realistic to assume that, as a farmer-entrepreneur, he had a long list of tasks that required his attention and time.

She peeked through the swinging door that led into the cafe's main room. Amanda, bless her heart, was at her usual spot behind the counter, her nose once again buried in a biology textbook. She'd make a wonderful nurse someday, caring and knowledge-able. For now, Holly was grateful to have her as part of the team.

Perhaps sensing Holly's presence, Amanda looked up. "Hey, boss."

"Hey," Holly replied. "It's quieting down. I'm going to get some fresh air."

"Okay, see you in a bit."

A few minutes later, bundled against the cold, Holly set out in the direction of Heartsprings Lake, her stride purposeful and energetic as she made her way through her beloved neighborhood. The sky overhead was clear and blue. Sun reflected brightly off the snow on the ground. The air carried a hint of evergreen. Down the block, she caught sight of kids in a high-spirited snowball fight, their peals of laughter bringing a smile to her lips. As always, the familiar sights and sounds comforted her, filling her with gratitude for her good fortune to be born and raised here.

As she approached the lake, she saw the usual

buzz of activity. Scores of townsfolk were taking advantage of the bright, crisp weather to enjoy the views and hit the ice. In the distance, at the outer edge of the ice, she noticed the man she'd seen two days earlier, the one skating with skill and purpose, the one who was using the ice to get in a good workout.

Only now, she recognized who it was: *Gabe.* She'd been struck by his athletic bearing at the cafe. Now, seeing him power across the ice, she saw that his appearance was matched by some serious skating skills.

At that moment, she heard a familiar voice call out, "Hey, Holly!"

Her head whipped around and she found herself gazing upon her friend Clara, sitting on a bench near the shore of the lake.

"Clara," Holly said, dashing over. "What brings you out here today?"

Her friend, who was slipping a winter boot onto her foot, pointed to a pair of skates on the ground beside her. "Just finished a whirl on the ice. How could I resist, on a day like this?"

"You got that right," Holly agreed. "A beautiful day."

"Crazy morning — tons going on — and I needed a breather."

"I know the feeling."

Holly looked fondly at her friend, who was, in a

word, adorable. An inch or so shorter than Holly, with shoulder-length light-brown hair and a cute face, she was a slim bundle of energy — an appealing combination of determination and cheerfulness. They hadn't known each other growing up — Clara was a decade younger and had left for New York the instant she graduated from high school — but they'd struck up a fast friendship after Clara moved back to Heartsprings Valley earlier that year. In her new job as town manager, working directly for Mayor Winters, Clara had reason to talk with Holly all the time. The job was a perfect fit for her, because Clara and the mayor were peas in a pod: both tireless town boosters and natural-born organizers.

Clara said, "Your daily power walk?"

Holly nodded.

"How's everything at the cafe?"

Her friend's tone was deliberately casual, but Holly knew instantly what she was really asking. "Everything's fine," she said evenly, not taking the bait. "How about you?"

"Oh, fine. Everything's fine." Clara's gaze wandered over Holly's shoulder toward the lake, her eyes widening as they locked in on something.

Unable to stop herself, Holly turned. Gabe was speeding across the ice toward them. When he saw them looking his way, he waved.

Unconsciously, Holly found herself waving back and gesturing for him to join them.

She flushed when she realized what she was doing and glanced at Clara, who was looking right at her. "Fine indeed," Clara murmured, a hint of a smile on her face.

"That's Gabe," Holly said, almost apologetically.

"The orchard guy?"

"You haven't met him?"

"Not yet. Bert mentioned him."

Of course he did, Holly thought. *What else had he mentioned?*

When Gabe reached the edge of the lake, he picked up a pair of blade covers and slipped them over his blades, one after the other. "Holly, good to see you!" he said as he strode up the shore toward them, a big grin on his face, his warm brown eyes aimed right at her.

"Great to see you, too," Holly said. "I'd like to introduce my friend Clara."

"Clara, nice to meet you," Gabe said, extending his gloved hand. "Gabe."

"Pleased to meet you," Clara replied.

Holly said, "Clara is the town manager — she works with Mayor Winters. Gabe is the new owner of Northland Orchard, right outside of town."

"The mayor's mentioned you," Clara said.

"He's been a huge help," Gabe said. "Full of ideas about how to meet folks and promote the orchard. I really appreciate everything he's done."

"He told me about the Wassail event you're having. Tomorrow night, right?"

"That's right. I hope you'll be able to attend."

"Count on it."

After a brief pause, Clara said, with a glance toward Holly, "I also hear you've set up a table at Holly's cafe to promote your new line of apple butters."

"The mayor suggested I ask." His gaze moved to Holly. "I'm glad I did."

Oh, my. Holly's cheeks flamed pink, and became even pinker when she realized what was happening. She really was going to have to find a way to *stop responding in such an unrealistic manner* when this man was around. She barely knew him, after all.

Desperate to change the subject, Holly gestured to his ice skates. "I didn't know you skated."

"Varsity hockey in college. Not quite good enough for the pros, but close."

"You look plenty good from what I can see."

Argh. Even as the words tumbled out, she was uncomfortably aware of the unintended double meaning.

"On the skates, I mean," she added. "The ice."

Gabe's eyebrows rose slightly. Clara's hand went to her mouth to cover a smile.

"Are you a skater?" Gabe asked Holly. "We should go sometime."

"Oh," she said. "Sure. I mean, yes. I mean, I skate. Not like you, but I'm okay."

Clara jumped in. "You could go right now."

"What do you mean?" Holly said.

"What's your size?"

"Eight."

"Same as me." Clara picked up her skates and handed them to a stunned Holly, then gestured to the bench. "See if they fit."

Holly gulped, her pulse racing as she realized there was no way to get out of trying on the skates without seeming rude. Besides, her inner voice was saying, *What the heck are you waiting for? Get your feet in those skates!*

She shot a glance at Gabe and shrugged. "If the skate fits…." She sat next to Clara on the bench, slipped off her right boot, took the skate, and slid her foot in.

She gulped again: It fit *perfectly*.

Clara grinned. "Look at that. Like it was meant to be." She handed Holly the other skate and stood up. "You two have fun. I'll swing by the cafe later to pick these up."

"You sure that's okay? I can bring them to you, if you'd like."

"No need. I won't be getting dinner till later tonight. Luke got roped into fixing up the bandstand for next week's Christmas concert, and he's busy at another job right now, which means he won't be getting to the bandstand until late, which means our dinner plans are getting pushed back — which is a long way of me saying that one of your cranberry-apple scones will be the perfect treat to tide me over till dinner."

Holly smiled. "I'll make sure we set one aside." She slipped into the second skate and stood up, wobbling a bit. She'd been a decent skater as a kid — no ice princess, but no slouch either — but it had been a while. "I'll try to return them in one piece."

She took a tentative step and wobbled again. Both Clara and Gabe reacted with alarm.

"You okay?" Gabe said, stepping closer.

From the concerned look on Clara's face, Holly sensed her friend was wondering if encouraging a skating adventure had been the right move.

Holly took another step, this one an improvement. "I think so."

"Here, take my arm," Gabe said, stepping next to her.

Clara nodded vigorously. "Yes, do that."

Yes, do that! Holly's inner voice agreed. "Thank you," she said. She took hold of Gabe's arm and immediately felt more secure. As anticipated, the arm was a good one — solid and muscular. The shoulder it was attached to was nice as well, and so was the —

She blinked when she realized where her overactive brain was going. She glanced at Clara and found her friend suppressing yet another smile.

"I'll leave you two to it," Clara said, a twinkle in her eye.

Even in the crisp air, Holly felt the red in her cheeks deepen. "Thank you. For the skates, I mean."

"Uh huh. See you later!"

Holly watched Clara's retreating figure, then turned her attention to Gabe, who was looking at her expectantly. There was curiosity in his gaze, perhaps even a hint of excitement.

"Ready?" he asked.

Involuntarily, her grip on his arm tightened. "Ready as I'll ever be."

CHAPTER 10

ogether they made their way down to the lake, his strength reassuring her as their blades crunched on the sandy shore. She hadn't been on the ice in a while — three or four years, she realized — and she'd never been all that skillful. Not terrible, but fully capable of an embarrassing tumble or two.

Please, she found herself fervently hoping, *please don't let me fall flat on my you-know-what.*

"You okay?" Gabe asked.

She gulped, realizing she'd perhaps been gripping his arm too tightly. "Sorry," she said, releasing him as they reached the edge of the lake.

Gabe slipped off his blade covers, stepped onto the ice, and turned toward her. "How are you feeling?" he asked.

"Good." She let out a short laugh. "Okay, honestly? A bit nervous. It's been a while."

"No rush. Take your time." He extended his hands. "Grab hold."

She reached out, her hands gripping his. Instantly, she responded to their solidity. She stepped on the ice and felt the blades slide smoothly beneath her.

"How's that feel?" he asked.

"Good." She moved one leg forward, then another, gliding forward hesitantly, comforted by the hands holding hers.

The ice seemed to flow beneath her as their skates glided over the frozen surface. Before she knew it, she and Gabe had floated away from the shore. She was now surrounded on all sides by an open expanse of white-grey ice. Out here, on the open lake, the brightness of the afternoon sun was dazzling. She felt the breeze pick up. Around them, other skaters dashed to and fro.

In front of her, Gabe was grinning at her, and she realized she was grinning back at him. Her shoulders began to loosen as she relaxed into the flow of movement.

"There you go," he said.

"It's been too long."

"You're a natural."

"Gosh, no. Hardly that." She realized they'd moved smoothly, even effortlessly, past the other skaters — past the kids playing hockey, parents with their kids, and couples skating together. They were out where she'd spotted Gabe the other day, when he was racing up and down the ice like the college hockey player he once was, pushing himself to work harder and go faster.

"I'm ready," she said.

"All right," he said, and let go.

With a surge of optimism, she launched herself forward, gradually building speed, her confidence increasing with every push and glide. She felt herself becoming a kid again, racing into the wind, skates flashing in the sun, daring the world to stop her.

"Look at you go!" Gabe yelled, watching her with admiration. "Go, Holly, go!"

She laughed, her movements starting to flow as muscle memory kicked in. She sensed Gabe behind her, racing to catch up. When he did, he adjusted his pace to match hers. Together they glided forward, side by side.

"No wonder you do this!" she yelled as she kept pushing forward.

He laughed. "You like?"

"I love it!"

Eventually, her breathing became ragged and she was forced to slow down. Speed-skating was quite a workout! Very carefully, she brought herself to a stop, her heart thumping away.

Gabe did two swift circles around her before

slicing to a graceful stop at her side. "You built up some speed there," he said with a grin.

Between breaths, she said, "I guess I did."

"I love it out here."

"I can see why."

"Been out here every day since the lake froze over."

"Every day?"

"My new daily break. My daily sanity check."

"I have one of those, too. A daily walk. Same reason."

The breeze picked up again and she welcomed its coolness on her heated cheeks. She heard the cry of a hawk above and looked up, searching the blue skies for it until she found it floating high above the ridge surrounding the lake.

Next to her, Gabe said, "Ideas flow when I'm out here."

"Ideas for the orchard?"

"Like the other day, I was in the middle of a speed drill when I figured out how to get controlled-atmosphere storage up and running before next fall's harvest."

From the way his face lit up, it was clear that "controlled-atmosphere storage" was important to him — but what was it, exactly? He'd mentioned the harvest, so the term probably had something to do with apples and how to store them....

He must have seen the puzzled look in her eyes.

"Sorry," he said. "Geeking out again. More jargon. More and more these days, farming is a high-tech enterprise."

"I don't know the term, but I'm guessing it's a way to store apples after the harvest?"

He nodded. "It's a specially built room that allows us to control temperature and oxygen levels. If we store apples in a low-oxygen, low-temperature environment, we can keep them fresh for months. Which means we can put them on the market year-round."

"Right now, you don't have one of these rooms?"

"Setting one up requires a substantial investment."

"Let me guess," Holly said. "The idea you came up with, out here on the ice, is to set one up cooperatively with other local farmers. All of you pitching in together to build it and operate it."

His brown eyes registered surprise. "That's right. But how did you...."

She waved her arms around. "Look at where we are. Makes perfect sense that you'd be inspired to think about your neighbors while you're out here."

He followed her arms, taking in the beautiful blue sky, the ridge line of snow-capped trees, and the happy crowd of skaters zooming over the ice. He laughed. "I hadn't made the connection, but you nailed it. This little town is proving quite the inspiration."

"If you don't mind my asking, what inspired you to leave New York and move up here?"

His gaze returned to her. "Three summers ago, I was up here with my ... ex-girlfriend. On an impulse, we stopped at a roadside apple stand and got to talking with the farmer. He mentioned an orchard tour up the road, and we decided to check it out."

Holly nodded, listening closely. He'd said *ex-girlfriend*, as in former girlfriend. But he'd paused as he said it. What did that pause mean? "So you went to the orchard and...?"

"Well, I guess you could say I got hooked." He shrugged, as if unable to believe what had happened. "Everything about the orchard spoke to me. Everything was completely fascinating. I asked a ton of questions — too many, according to Carrie. I couldn't stop talking about it. My interest didn't fade when we got back to New York. If anything, I became even more serious, even more focused. It took me about a year to figure out how, but I came up with a plan to make it work and then...."

"And then you did it."

"I made the leap. Dived right in. Bought an orchard, quit my job, and moved up here."

"Spoken like a true entrepreneur."

He smiled wryly. "You mean, true obsessive."

"Absolutely," she replied, smiling back. "I think you have to be a little bit crazy to launch a business. Starting the cafe was like nothing I'd ever done before. All-consuming. More work than I ever imagined. Especially the first couple of years."

"But worth it?"

"Definitely," she said, a sense of pride stirring within her. "Looking back, I wouldn't trade the experience for anything. I love my cafe, and my team, and my customers."

He exhaled, like her words were a relief to him. "I'm glad to hear that. I've been at this just under a year now. I hope in a few years I can say the same."

"I'm sure you can and will."

The breeze picked up a bit, carrying with it a hint of evergreen from the trees blanketing the ridge along the lake. The sun overhead, still bright, was nonetheless beginning its daily descent. It was time to head to shore and get back to the cafe.

But not quite yet. She knew she was being nosy, but she couldn't help herself. "And … your ex-girlfriend? How did she feel about you starting a business?"

He frowned, then sighed. "She tried to be supportive, and we both tried to be flexible, but in the end, we couldn't make it work. It came down to a simple, painful reality at the end of the day: I wanted to be farmer and she didn't. She's a city girl at heart."

"That must have been hard."

"It was. For both of us. Our life goals were just too different."

Holly gave him a sympathetic smile. "Are you still in touch?"

He shook his head. "Not really, no. It's been a while. I hear about her occasionally from friends."

"Do you miss her?"

He went still as he considered her question, his gaze fixed downward on the grey ice beneath their skates. Then he raised his warm eyes to meet hers. "I did at first, but lately ... no."

His gaze seemed to grow more intense.

She felt a flush spread up her cheeks.

"Lately," he said, "not at all."

CHAPTER 11

Oh, my. Her pulse picked up. Not the answer she was expecting. Not in the least. He was so — direct. No hesitation about saying it. None at all.

"I see," she said, trying to keep her tone light as she desperately prayed for her pink cheeks to settle down. "That's good, right? Helps you focus on the orchard?"

"Right," he said. "The orchard." He blinked, as if suddenly remembering he had an orchard. "Speaking of, do we need to get back to the cafe?"

She peeked under her glove at her watch. "Oh, gosh. Amanda and George will be expecting me."

Together, they glided their way back to the shore. Her movements across the ice felt sure and smooth now, her earlier nervousness gone. Funny how a bit of experience could make such a difference. When they reached the edge, Gabe slipped on his blade covers and walked with her up the sandy shore to the bench where she'd left her boots.

"If you'd like, I can give you a ride back," he said as she slipped back into her boots.

"Thanks." She stood up, skates in hand, and walked with him to his truck, the snow on the ground crunching softly beneath them. Her earlier sense of awkwardness had snuck up on her again. Out on the ice, the conversation had flowed. But now, back on solid ground, it felt like she was returning to reality.

Gabe, perhaps sensing the same, pointed to a dark blue truck. "There," he said. As they got closer, she saw "Northland Orchard" stenciled in crisp white lettering on the side door along with a phone number, address and website, the typography matching the labeling for his apple butters.

"I really like what you're doing with your branding," she said.

"Thanks." He pointed to her skates. "Here, let me take those."

She handed him the skates. He set them in the truck bed, took off his skates, grabbed his boots from the back of the truck, and slipped them on while she made her way to the passenger side of the truck.

"You ready?" he said.

"Yep." She opened the door and climbed in,

settling into the bench seat next to a folder filled with papers.

He hopped in on the driver's side and moved the folder closer to him. "Sorry about that. My to-do list. I carry it with me everywhere."

She noticed a town map peeking out from the top of the folder. "I see you got yourself the local map."

"An essential guide," he said as he started up, the engine catching immediately and giving a throaty rumble.

"Mind if I...?"

He nodded and she pulled out the map. Originally produced decades earlier and now updated regularly by the town council, the map showed every nook and cranny of Heartsprings Valley and its surroundings — every street, park, trail, and local landmark. Her eyes scanned the familiar terrain, zooming in on her house and then her cafe.

With a glance over his shoulder to make sure all was clear, Gabe slowly backed out. "Even though I've been here close to a year, I still feel like I've barely scratched the surface of this place."

"It takes a while."

"You're a native, right? Born and raised?"

"That's right," she said, wondering how he'd known that before immediately realizing that —

"Your mom mentioned that," he said.

Of course her mom had mentioned that. *Along with what else?* "It was a great place to be a kid."

"Is it a great place for adults?" he asked, throwing her a grin as he turned onto the road.

"It's a great place for adults, too," she replied, smiling back.

"What's the dating scene like?"

She blinked. Talk about a *minefield*. He was so direct! Mostly, that was a very good thing. But maybe not when his questions caught her flat-footed, like right this very instant?

"Um…," she said, stalling for time.

"Like, how did you meet the guy you're dating?" he asked, glancing at her briefly before fixing his eyes on the road. A flush appeared on his cheeks, almost like he felt self-conscious.

The air in the truck heated up. She suddenly felt very warm.

"Sorry. Didn't mean to pry. I mean" — he looked over, almost apologetically — "we've just started getting to know each other."

"Oh, no worries," she said, relieved at how level and calm she sounded. She took a deep breath. "Actually, I'm not dating anyone right now."

"Ah," he said, excitement flashing in his eyes.

"Unless you count the cafe."

He laughed.

"Sometimes I feel I'm definitely married to my job."

He laughed again. "Ditto." He pointed ahead. "Speaking of…."

They'd reached the town square, the cafe just ahead. Gabe found a spot across the street and parked, then turned to her. "Here we are."

"Here we are indeed," she said, her hand reaching for the door handle but not quite finding it. With his attention fixed on her, his strong shoulders turned toward her, she became aware of herself hesitating, lingering. She felt an impulse to remain right there, in the moment, to draw out the mood, the hint, the whatever-you-want-to-call-it building between them.

They blinked simultaneously, as if being plucked from their own little bubble. "Guess we should get in there," he said with a hint of reluctance.

"Guess so," she said, then pushed open the door and let the crisp winter air flow over her. She hopped out, grabbed Clara's skates from the back of the truck, and, after glancing both ways for traffic, scooted with Gabe across the street to the cafe.

The door's tinkling bell welcomed them as she stepped in. The convivial chatter and bustle inside warmed her heart. Most of the seats and tables in the cafe were occupied, with a line of customers keeping Amanda busy at the counter. Amanda glanced over and waved at Holly.

A woman approached Gabe. "Hi. I hear you're the new owner of the orchard?"

"That's right," he said, then turned to Holly. "I should probably...."

"Absolutely," Holly said. "Talk to you in a bit." As Gabe turned his attention to the customer, Holly joined Amanda behind the counter. "How's everything?" she asked her protégé.

"Good," Amanda said as she rang up an order. "Doing great business today."

"Everything okay out here?"

"Fine. Bev called. She'll be here in a bit."

"Good. Let me check in on George." Stepping through the swinging doors into the kitchen, Holly found her indispensable line cook scrubbing the sink.

George glanced over at her, then at the clock on the wall. "How was the lake?" he asked.

"Great," she said.

He noticed the skates in her arms. "What's with those?"

"They're Clara's. She'll swing by to pick them up later."

"You went skating?"

"I did. It was such a beautiful day."

"Took a longer break than usual."

"Guess I lost track of time, out there on the ice."

"And you came in from the front."

"That's right."

"You always come in from the back."

She felt her cheeks begin to flush yet again. "I got a ride."

He gave her a frank, no-nonsense look. She knew what he was thinking: *Gabe is changing things here.*

George wasn't wrong. And she was okay with that — as long as she stayed grounded. She'd be fine as long as she avoided falling prey to unrealistic flights of fancy.

"Yes," she said. "Gabe was there, too, and he gave me a ride back. He's out front now, at his table."

With a frown, George returned his attention to the sink, giving it a final scrub before rinsing the sponge and his hands while Holly hung up her coat on the hook near the door.

"Everything's fine," she reassured him. "Promise."

George dried his hands, then joined her at the coat rack and shrugged into his parka. "If you say so, boss." He gestured toward the counter. "New pie out twenty minutes ago."

"He's actually a very nice guy. Have you met him?"

Hand on the back door handle, George paused. "Good idea."

Holly blinked. Before she could say another word, George turned and marched into the front room. She hurried after him and peeked through the swinging door as the two men shook hands and started talking. Over the hubbub of conversation, she couldn't make out what they were saying, but when Gabe picked up a jar of apple butter and handed it to George, she let out a sigh and returned to the kitchen, where a long to-do list awaited her.

Everything was going to be fine. George had no cause to worry. Once the Christmas rush was over, Gabe and his table would be gone. He'd return to his orchard, and her cafe would return to its normal state.

And that was what she wanted, right? A return to normal.

Right?

Wrong, she heard her heart whisper. *Very, very wrong!*

CHAPTER 12

That evening, long after the last customer headed out into the night, long after she flipped the sign on the cafe door from "Open" to "Closed," long after Gabe returned to the orchard to tackle his own long list of chores, long after her mom dashed home to get dinner ready, Holly kept the oven busy in the kitchen. She was, she acknowledged to herself, a woman on a mission: to incorporate Northland Orchard's line of apple butters into her Heartsprings Valley cookbook. The book was meant to celebrate and honor her hometown, after all, and with Gabe and the orchard now part of the community, the fruits of his labors deserved to be included.

She just had to figure out how. With a puzzled frown, she stared at the four jars of apple butter lined up on the kitchen counter, working through her plan of attack. Three of the jars featured a single type of apple, two of which she was familiar with (McIntosh and Baldwin) and one she was not (Blushing Golden). The fourth jar of apple butter blended the three apples together.

First things first: taste tests. She opened each jar, grabbed a spoon, and gave each a try, allowing the flavors and textures to roll over her tongue. All were wonderfully caramelized, she was relieved to find, but their flavors differed in important ways.

The Northland Orchard Cinnamon Apple Butter, which used Baldwin apples, captured the spicy sweet-tart taste of the Baldwin and complemented it with a dash of cinnamon. The Northland Orchard Creamy Apple Butter, which featured McIntosh apples, offered the apple's distinctively smooth sweet-tart flavor. The third butter, Northland Orchard Sweet Apple Butter, was the sweetest of the bunch, which Holly guessed was due partly to the Blushing Golden's natural sweetness, along with the hints of honey and lavender that Gabe had added.

The most intriguing of the four was the Northland Orchard Classic Apple Butter, which combined all three apples together. It was perhaps the most quintessentially apple-like of the four butters, announcing its essence with quiet, simple pride — the flavor initially quite tart, but with a richness that lingered. She scooped up a second spoonful, allowing her mind to wander as she teased out the tastes, knowing from past experience that inspiration would arrive when it was ready and not before.

As her subconscious hummed along, she turned her attention to how the apple butters might fit in with the cafe's menu. All of them would work wonderfully as spreads for her scones, muffins, and breads, and it would be easy enough to come up with the right pairings to match the right apple butter and the right treat.

But that really wasn't enough. On an impulse, she went to her desk, grabbed her folder of recipes, and opened it to the still-unfinished recipe for her not-yet-perfect bacon scone. Her mom had suggested adding a hint of sweetness. What if she tried apple butter?

Satisfied with that idea, she got to work, quickly combining the dry ingredients — flour, sugar, baking powder, salt, and a dash of spice — into a big bowl and then using a fork to mix in the butter until the dough arrived at the desired crumbly consistency. On the radio, the local station started playing a jaunty, big-band version of "Jingle Bells." She sang along as she turned her attention to the wet ingredients. Using four different bowls — one for each apple butter — she whisked eggs, apple butter, and vanilla in each, then added the dry ingredients and stirred. When the doughs had the right amount of stickiness, she folded in bacon.

She nodded, satisfied, then grabbed two big

baking sheets and, after lining them with parchment paper, sliced and arranged the dough on the two trays. To help her remember which dough had which apple butter, she lined up the jars in order next to the oven.

The dough needed to chill, so she took the two sheets to the freezer, slid them in, set the timer for twenty minutes, then turned around and swept her gaze over the kitchen. She had a million things to do — she always did — so how best to use the time? The possibilities were endless. She had mail to sort through, bills to pay, inventory to order, dishes to clean, counters to scrub, tables to wipe — the list went on and on.

But curiosity won out. With no small measure of exasperation with herself, she found herself walking across the kitchen to her small desk, opening her laptop, and typing "Northland Orchard" into the search engine. When the results yielded the orchard's website, excitement fluttered through her. She clicked the link and was pleased to find that the site was well-designed, with beautiful photos of the orchard and information about the orchard's products presented in a clear, professional manner.

She was glad the orchard's website was good. *As a neighbor, you have a friendly interest in Gabe's business succeeding,* she tried to tell herself.

Ha ha, nice try, shot back her inner truth-teller. *A*

good website shows he's smart, and you want him to be smart.

The photos captured the farm's rolling hills in their autumn glory and the orchard's apples at their ripest and most tempting. She leaned in to examine a shot of Gabe and his team standing proudly with bushels of apples in front of a large white two-story farmhouse. Gabe looked happy standing there, his strong arms holding a basket full of red apples. Her attention wandered to the house behind him, which was wide and tall, probably dating back a century, with clapboard siding and a big front porch. Had she ever been inside that house as a kid? She didn't think so — she hadn't known the previous owners. Which meant at least one part of Heartsprings Valley remained a mystery to her. The porch prevented her from seeing much about the rooms inside — what she imagined were the living room, dining room, and kitchen.

She wanted to find more pictures of the farmhouse — surely more were just a click or two away — but she resisted the urge. The Wassail event was the following evening. She'd see more — and satisfy her curiosity — soon enough. She eyed the stack of mail next to the laptop and sighed. There were bills that needed paying. Right now would be an excellent time to do just that and act like the responsible, mature, realistic businesswoman she was.

She glanced at the clock. In twelve minutes, when

the pieces of dough were properly chilled, she'd brush them with milk, sprinkle on turbinado sugar, and get them into the oven. If she was lucky, the scones would turn out delicious. If she was even luckier, one of the apple butters would emerge as the winning ingredient.

Filled with resolve, she tore open the electric bill. Yes, time to put her head on straight. She was going to pay bills. Bake scones.

And avoid looking at more farmhouse photos!

CHAPTER 13

*T*he next day flew by in a flurry, with a constant stream of customers keeping Holly, her mom, Amanda, and George hopping from the moment the cafe opened its doors. In addition to the regulars who made up most of their business, the cafe filled up with folks placing orders for holiday parties, and shoppers loaded with bags of Christmas gifts who wanted — needed — a caffeine fix and a scone to power them through the rest of their busy day. The sound of conversation and laughter warmed Holly's heart and kept her spirits high as she whipped up batch after batch of baked goods for the hungry throng.

Inevitably, as the late-afternoon sun disappeared below the horizon, the energy lessened as customers ventured back to their shopping. George and Amanda, who had both stayed an hour later than usual, headed home and would join Holly and her mom later at the Wassail event — George with his wife Millie, and Amanda with her sister Eva.

As for Gabe, he'd called that morning. "Sorry I can't make it to the cafe today. A lot to do to get everything set up and ready out here."

"Totally understand," Holly had replied. "My mom and I will head over early to help with last-minute setup. See you then!"

"Really appreciate it. Looking forward to it."

His voice had sounded so genuine. She gave the kitchen island a final wipe, the stainless-steel surface gleaming. Indeed, everything about Gabriel North struck her as warm and real. He was direct and focused, observant and appreciative. If he wanted something, he went for it — his new career as apple farmer proved that. She felt a tingle of anticipation as she realized she would soon get to see his orchard — his dream, his business, his passion — up close and in person.

She'd already packed up a box of taste-test scones she'd made with Gabe's apple butters. In her view, one of the scones was the clear winner and her mom agreed, but she was curious what Gabe would think. She dashed into the bathroom to give herself a final visual check — yes, the burgundy sweater she'd picked this morning had proved a good choice for her black slacks. She collected her winter coat, gloves, scarf, and handbag, ran her eyes over the kitchen a final time to make sure she hadn't forgotten anything, then turned off the light and headed through the swinging doors into the front, where her mom was wrapping up a different box of scones.

"Anything I can help with?" Holly asked.

"Almost done," her mom said as she closed the lid and taped it shut. "There!" She set the box on the counter next to Gabe's box and grabbed her coat from the rack. "We'll swing by Abby's on the way."

As Holly picked up both boxes, the cafe's phone rang. Her mom reached for it. "Heartsprings Valley Cafe, Bev speaking." She listened for a moment. "Oh, my," she said. "Are you okay?" After listening some more, she added, "Well, I'm glad you're okay. And don't you worry — I'll be here when you get here."

Her mom hung up the phone and turned to Holly. "Darn."

"What is it?" Holly asked.

"That was Bill. I forgot about the delivery. His truck hit an icy patch and slid off the road. He's waiting for a tow to yank him out."

Holly felt a jolt. She'd forgotten about the delivery as well, which wasn't like her. The delivery included much-needed cafe supplies — coffee cups, stirrers, napkins, and other daily essentials. "Is he okay? He's not hurt, is he?"

"No, he's fine and his truck's fine, but he's stuck, so he'll be here later than usual."

Holly sighed, set the boxes down, and began unwrapping her scarf. "I'll wait for him."

Her mom shook her head. "No, I'll wait. You go ahead."

Holly's eyes widened. "Why you?"

"Because I'm perfectly able to wait for him. I'll be fine," her mom said, her tone firm.

"You want me to go to the orchard without you?"

Her mom handed Holly the key to her car. "I'm sure you can manage."

If Holly hadn't just seen the call come in, if she hadn't just heard her mom's conversation with Bill, she would have suspected motherly shenanigans. But no, this time the only hint of maternal maneuvering was her mom volunteering to stay behind to wait for the delivery.

Holly frowned. "Of course I can manage getting there on my own, but what about you? How will you get there?"

Her mom was already unbuttoning her coat. "Your dad will pick me up. We'll join you as soon as we can."

And that seemed to be all there was to say about that. "You sure?"

Her mom handed her the two boxes of scones. "Go, dear. See you soon. Be sure to bring the top box to Abby's first."

Holly leaned over and gave her mom a peck on the cheek. "See you in a bit."

"Drive safely, dear. Watch out for icy patches."

Her mom's car was parked nearby, so Holly chose to walk across the square to Abby's store, Chocolate Heaven, with the boxes of scones in her arms. The night air was always cold this time of year, but the breeze this evening was soft. As she passed the bandstand in the center of the square, she paused to admire the holiday lights outlining its edges. In a few evenings, the town's annual Christmas caroling concert would take place in this very spot. She smiled as memories of previous concerts rushed through her. Unable to stop herself, she started humming one of her favorite tunes, agreeing with the song's lyrics that it was beginning to look a lot like a certain time of year.

When she got to Abby's store, she pushed open the door and, as always, was enveloped in chocolate-scented warmth.

From behind the counter, Abby gave her a welcoming smile. "Holly, so good to see you." Beneath her white apron, she was wearing a green-and-white sweater depicting a snow-covered evergreen forest.

"You, too," Holly replied.

Abby spied the box in Holly's hands. "Are those what I think they are?"

Holly grinned. "The one on top is special delivery, just for you."

"Perfect." Abby accepted the box, her eyes alive with pleasure.

Holly bent down in front of the display counter, admiring the exquisite chocolate treats that Abby made by hand in the back. "I could stare at these all day. They're almost too beautiful to eat."

"I have something for you to bring to the orchard."

Holly stood up. "What's that?"

Abby handed her a wrapped box of chocolates, which Holly knew from extensive personal experience contained two dozen of Abby's finest nougats, truffles, and more. "Gabriel is holding a raffle for the Christmas charity drive, and this is one of the prizes."

"Perfect," Holly said. "I promise I'll try really hard to resist the temptation to open this box and devour every single piece in it."

Abby laughed and handed Holly a sample chocolate-caramel nougat. "Perhaps this will tide you over."

"Oh gosh — thank you." Holly took the nougat eagerly and bit in. "Mmm, my favorite," she said, loving the richness of the chocolate and caramel flowing over her taste buds.

Abby smiled, pleased to have a fan. "I like our new neighbor."

Between chews, Holly said, "You've met him?"

"He came in several times over the summer — he

likes chocolates, too — but I didn't actually get to know him until recently, when Bert introduced him."

"I just met him, too."

"How's it going, him having a table at the cafe?"

"Good," Holly said. "Fine." Inwardly, she sighed. Of course, everyone in town knew that Gabe had set up a table in her cafe. Of course, everyone was curious.

"I have a good feeling about him," Abby said. "I think he'll fit in well here."

Holly nodded, aware of what Abby was really suggesting — that Gabe would fit well with *Holly* — but choosing to not reply. Folks in this town were incorrigible when it came to matchmaking. Instead, she set the chocolates on top of the box of scones and said, "Will you be at the Wassail event this evening?"

Abby shook her head regretfully. "Unfortunately, no. But please give Gabriel my best."

"I'll do that," Holly replied, then turned to head back out. "Merry Christmas!"

"Merry Christmas!" Abby said.

CHAPTER 14

*M*inutes later, Holly hopped into her mom's car, set the boxes of scones and chocolates on the passenger seat, turned the key in the ignition, and felt the engine rumble to life. After buckling in and pushing the seat back a couple of notches — she needed a bit more leg room than her mom — she headed out of town into the heart of the valley. With the car heater on high and the radio blasting "All I Want for Christmas Is You," she sang along as her neighbors' homes and farms flowed by, the familiar music and Christmas decorations and the army of snowmen — Heartsprings Valley loved its snowmen — lifting her spirits. Northland Orchard was about fifteen minutes away, nestled at the base of Heartsprings Ridge. She recalled being there once or twice as a kid during the autumn harvests, but her memories of the place were hazy at best.

A few minutes outside of town, she turned off the valley's main road and headed down a winding lane, her headlights playing across the fields, the snow-topped fenceposts marking her progress. Soon enough, spring would arrive and the fields would once again burst with the hay and sweet corn that farmers coaxed from the valley's soil. But for now, the fields lay fallow, patiently waiting for winter to pass.

The lane's dips and curves required her careful attention, so she slowed and focused. She'd always been a decent driver, but living a short walk from the cafe meant that she often went days without driving, and it was easy to fall out of practice. As she hugged a bend, she noticed her mom's Santa Claus ornament swinging gently from the rear-view mirror. A smile came to her lips. Her mom loved her rear-view mirror decorations and was always updating them to reflect the time of year: something with hearts for Valentine's Day, red-white-and-blue for the Fourth of July, scary-funny for Halloween, turkey-related for Thanksgiving, and of course Christmas-related for her favorite holiday of the year.

Up ahead, the lane began to gently rise. She was getting close to the orchard. Her headlights caught a row of apple trees, branches bare as they hunkered down for winter, followed by another row of trees and then another.

She topped a crest and caught her first glimpse of

the farmhouse up ahead, its white clapboard siding sporting Christmas lights twinkling merrily in the darkness. She passed a wooden sign that read "Welcome to Northland Orchard" in the same distinctive lettering she'd seen on Gabe's apple butter jars.

The lane ended in a wide, well-lit gravel parking area in front of the farmhouse. Several cars and trucks were already parked there, including Gabe's. Holly pulled in next to his and took a deep breath as anxiety fluttered through her. She turned on the overhead car light and aimed the rear-view mirror at her face. Yes, her lips needed a touchup. She reached into her handbag, eventually finding her lip gloss, which she pulled out and applied. Was anything else in need of attention? Her cheeks looked — fine. Her eyeliner — acceptable. Her hair — barely acceptable. With a deep breath, she returned the lip gloss to her bag and turned off the overhead light. Wrapping her scarf snugly against her neck, she grabbed the boxes of scones and chocolates and eased out of the car.

The night air was cold but clear, her breath forming a fog. She heard the indistinct murmur of people talking inside the big red barn. Like the white clapboard farmhouse, the barn bordered the parking area. Next to the barn was a third building, a smaller wooden structure with a front porch, painted the same deep red as the barn, with a sign atop the porch that read, "Northland Orchard General Store."

Hesitantly, she made her way to the barn entrance

and peeked inside the half-opened doors. Her eyes widened. Looking upward, she saw the familiar wooden beams and rafters of a century-old barn. But at ground level, she found herself gazing upon a modern space, one apparently designed to meet the needs of a twenty-first-century apple farm. The stalls and hay were gone, the dirt floor replaced with concrete. The space had excellent lighting. Row upon row of gleaming aluminum barrels lined the walls. In the center of the barn stood machines whose purposes she could only guess at. Instead of the ever-familiar smells of cut hay and animals, she caught a hint of fresh cider.

On the opposite side of the barn, the back doors were open to the night, and it was there she spied Gabe in conversation with a man who held the reins of a gray-white horse with a snowy white mane and tail. She made her way through the barn toward the two men, unable to tear her eyes from the beautiful animal, who noticed her approach and gently snorted a greeting.

The man talking to Gabe heard the horse's snort and glanced in Holly's direction. "Gabe," he said, "a visitor."

Gabe turned around and a big smile appeared on his handsome face. "Holly. Welcome!"

"Hi," Holly said as she quickened her pace.

Gabe was dressed in jeans, boots, red plaid shirt and mackinaw — his usual ensemble, she suspected.

His eyes were alive with pleasure at seeing her. He gave her a quick but awkward hug — the boxes in her arms were in the way — then said, "Here, let me help you with those."

"Thanks," she said, letting him take the boxes, which he set atop a nearby aluminum barrel. "That's a box of chocolates from Abby, along with scones from the cafe."

"Great." He gestured to the other man. "Holly, do you know Jeremiah?"

"No," she said, extending her hand. "Pleased to meet you."

"Likewise," Jeremiah said, taking her hand in his. He was in his forties, stocky and short, with a trimmed brown beard and a round face built for smiling. Like Gabe, he was dressed in outdoor gear.

Gabe said, "Holly owns and runs the Heart-springs Valley Cafe in the center of town."

"Ah," Jeremiah said. "My wife Nancy works part-time at the bookstore, so she's in your cafe all the time."

"Oh!" Holly said with a grin. "I love Nancy. She always has such great recommendations for new books."

"She loves your cafe," Jeremiah replied with a chuckle. "Especially your cranberry-apple scones. She raves about 'em."

Holly blushed. "I'm so glad to hear that."

"Jeremiah lives two farms down," Gabe said,

"and he offered to make Bessie available tonight for the kids."

Holly's gaze slid toward the horse, whose kind eyes regarded her with curiosity and patience. "Okay if I say hi?"

Jeremiah chuckled. "Please do."

With rising excitement, Holly held out her hand for the horse to sniff with her sensitive nose. Bessie snorted a greeting and Holly stepped closer to stroke her flank. As always in the presence of a horse, she found herself bewitched, the soft hair almost magical to the touch. "She's so beautiful," Holly said reverently. "I've loved horses since I was a little girl. For as long as I can remember."

Jeremiah nodded. "Bessie's about as sweet and gentle as they come."

"I'm sure the kids will love her."

"Definitely," Gabe agreed. "Especially when they see what else Jeremiah brought." He pointed to a spot outside the back of the barn and stepped aside to let her see —

Holly gasped. A one-horse open sleigh!

"I can't believe it," she said.

Gabe said, "One of Jeremiah's hobbies is restoring old treasures."

"Got this one at an estate sale," Jeremiah said. "An honest-to-goodness Portland Cutter, dating back to the 1890s. She was plenty beat up, but as soon as I laid eyes on her, I knew she had a lot of life left in her."

Holly's eyes feasted on Jeremiah's find. Everything about the sleigh gleamed and beckoned. The curved body was painted a bold, shiny red, with an evergreen motif carefully applied to each side. From the back hung a row of bells that Holly knew would jingle brightly. The runners supporting the sleigh — or maybe they were the blades, she supposed, not sure what to call them — were painted black and looked strong and sleek. She stepped closer and ran her hand over the bench's red tufted upholstery — water-resistant leather, from the feel of it — marveling at Jeremiah's attention to detail.

"I'm so impressed," Holly breathed. "I can't believe how beautiful this is."

"Thanks," Jeremiah replied.

"The best part," Gabe added, "is it's fully operational."

"Bessie can pull it?"

Jeremiah nodded. "On short, flat courses, absolutely."

Gabe said, "Earlier today, we packed down snow on a course through the orchard." He turned to Jeremiah. "How about taking Holly on a test drive?"

Jeremiah grinned, his gaze wandering from Gabe to Holly and back. "Great idea. Why don't you take the reins?"

Gabe's eyebrows rose. "For real?"

"You did great earlier today. I'll get Bessie hitched up."

Gabe turned to Holly, excitement in his eyes. "How about a sleigh ride through the orchard?"

"Are you sure?" she said with a mixture of surprise, anxiety, and pleasure. "Right now?"

"Right now." He held out his hand, and Holly, with a quick intake of breath, reached out and took it. His grip, strong and reassuring, felt instinctively right. Gabe helped her into the sleigh. Up front, Jeremiah led Bessie to the carriage and got her hitched up.

Holly settled into the cushioned bench, scooting over to make sure Gabe had plenty of room.

"What am I forgetting?" Gabe said to Jeremiah.

Jeremiah glanced over. "Blankets. I'll get them in a sec."

"Thanks," Gabe said, then turned to Holly. "How are you feeling?"

"Great," she replied, which was true — though if she were being completely honest, she would have included "nervous" and "unsettled" in her answer.

"It's a short ride. We're thinking folks will enjoy it."

"Absolutely."

Up front, Jeremiah adjusted a strap and nodded, satisfied. He patted Bessie's dappled hindquarters and said softly, "You ready to show what you can do, girl?" Bessie snorted in the affirmative and Jeremiah handed Gabe the reins. "She's eager to get out there. Remember, when you get to the turn, she'll want to do it herself. Hang on a sec while I get the blankets." From a basket near the barn door, he pulled out two red-tartan wool blankets and handed them to Gabe.

"Thanks," Gabe said, then turned to Holly. "Let's get these over our legs."

She helped him lay the blankets atop them. Gabe waited for her to tuck herself in, then said, "You ready?"

For just a split second, Holly paused to take all this in. Here she was, in a lovingly restored one-horse open sleigh. With a beautiful, gentle horse. In an apple orchard. Beneath the stars on a cold, clear night. Next to a man she'd met only a few days ago.

A man she wanted to know so much better.

A man who was waiting for her to answer.

"Yes," she exhaled.

Gabe grinned and gently flicked the reins. Bessie, with a burst of energy, pressed forward.

And they were off!

Holly gasped as the sleigh slid easily over the packed snow. Acting like she'd done it a million times, the horse aimed for the flattened path between two rows of apple trees, the steady crunch of her hooves on the hard-packed snow reassuring Holly that the horse knew exactly what she was doing.

She glanced at Gabe, who was already looking at her, grinning.

"This is wonderful," she breathed.

The crisp air flowed over her cheeks as Bessie pulled the sleigh past trees whose snow-covered branches almost glowed in the dark. There was movement in the sleigh, every *clomp-clomp-clomp* vibrating through her, every little bump in the snow jostling her to and fro as the bells jingled merrily.

Next to her, Gabe held the reins with assurance, his attention focused on the horse and the path ahead.

"Doing pretty good for a city slicker," she said mischievously.

He grinned in mock-protest. "My city-slicking days are behind me. I'm a man of the earth now."

She laughed. "Good with horses, too."

"That's easy with a gal like Bessie. She's a sweetheart."

Up front, almost as if she were listening, Bessie snorted in agreement.

Holly laughed again. "Yes, Bessie, you certainly are a sweetheart. And gorgeous to boot." She was glad they had the blankets covering their legs — already she was warming up, thanks to the protection the wool offered from the cold night air.

Her gaze wandered toward the trees they were passing, branches bare, waiting for the return of spring. "I think you mentioned this, but how many acres do you have?"

"Just under twenty. Which makes us a small orchard."

"Is small good? Does that mean more manageable?"

He nodded. "Generally, yes, smaller means easier to manage. But it also means we have to be smarter and more focused."

"In terms of what you grow?"

"Yep, and in terms of what and how we harvest, produce, and market." He gestured ahead, to a turn in the path. "The turn is the tricky part of this. How's the ride so far?"

"Oh, it's great."

"Okay for kids?"

"They'll love it."

Up ahead, the path curved left and then ran between another row of trees back to the barn. "All right," Gabe said when they reached the turn, "here goes." He gave the rein a twitch and Bessie, who clearly knew exactly what to do, pushed her left shoulder against the sleigh's shaft, crossed her front legs, and bore down, basically spinning the sleigh behind her over the hard-packed snow.

"Wow," Holly breathed. "What a horse!"

Gabe grinned. "Good job, Bessie!"

Bessie neighed in agreement. Turn accomplished, she set out at a confident trot back toward the barn.

"I'd say the test drive is a success," Gabe said.

Holly nodded. "Most definitely."

The sleigh hit a bump in the path, pushing Holly against Gabe. Immediately, her attention zoomed in on her shoulder pressing against Gabe's upper arm. Really, the right thing to do was to shift back to where she'd been — to break contact and give Gabe the space he might need to handle the reins freely and without interference. Really, that was what she should do.

Yet she found herself not moving an inch. Almost like her body wasn't listening to the rational, common-sense part of her brain. Almost like her arm and shoulder were glued to him. Stuck, immovable, fastened tight. Though not frozen, because if anything, her arm felt very warm!

For his part, Gabe didn't seem to mind her shoulder. He seemed to subtly lean in, as if he welcomed her presence there.

In silence, as if they were both secretly conspiring for the moment to last, they remained gently pressed together, the tinkling bells and crunching hooves accompanying them as the sleigh dashed through the still, crisp night. All too soon, Bessie's confident clomps brought them back to the barn, where Jeremiah awaited their return.

"So how was it? How'd she do?" he asked as he took the reins from Gabe.

"Great," Gabe said, then glanced at Holly. "And so was the ride." His gaze seemed to intensify. "Couldn't have asked for a better riding partner."

Holly blinked and nodded quickly, hoping the two men couldn't see the sudden flush of pink on her cheeks. "I had fun, too."

Gabe stepped out of the sleigh and helped her down, the feel of his hand in hers once again causing a flutter in her chest.

Jeremiah began unhitching the horse from the sleigh. "So about the event. Things starting soon?"

Gabe glanced at his watch. "About half an hour."

"Good," Jeremiah said. "Time to get my girl fed and watered." He finished unhitching the horse. "Don't you worry — Bessie and I got this part of the night's entertainment covered."

Gabe grinned. "Thanks, Jeremiah. Really appreciate it."

He and Holly watched him lead Bessie through the barn back to their trailer in the parking area.

Gabe turned to her and rubbed his hands together. "So," he said, "how about I give you a private tour before folks arrive?"

CHAPTER 15

a private tour? Just him and her? Holly's heart rate quickened. "I'd love that."

"Great," Gabe said. He seemed happy, even relieved, that she wanted to see more of the orchard. Almost like he wanted Holly to have an interest. Almost like her interest was important to him....

Don't get ahead of yourself, she cautioned.

"So about the apple trees," she said to focus herself. "When do they start growing apples, and when do you harvest them?"

"The apples appear in the spring — late March, early April," he said. "Harvest starts late summer and runs into early November, depending on apple type."

"And harvest is your busy season."

"Crazy-busy. I barely left the farm for two months. There was so much to do."

"Especially with it being your first year here."

He gave her a rueful nod. "Learning through doing. I started keeping a running list of all the mistakes I made."

"I do the same. Helps me avoid repeats."

"Hopefully."

"The way I see it, there's not enough time in the day to repeat a mistake, not with all the new mistakes I'm going to make."

He laughed. "Exactly."

"Well," she said with a shiver, wrapping her arms against the cold, "what do you do when the apples are harvested?"

He noticed her shivering and frowned. "You're cold."

"No, I'm fine."

He gestured to the barn. "How about we head inside, where it's warmer? I can show you a bit about the harvesting in there."

She nodded, ready for a break from the frigid night air. Together, they stepped into the comparative warmth of the barn.

"I can get one of the blankets from the sleigh, if you'd like."

"Oh, no. I'm fine. I grew up here, remember?"

He grinned. "If you say so."

"I do. Now, about the apple harvest. Treat me like I don't anything about how cider is produced, because I don't."

"Okay." He clapped his hands together again and looked at her like he was about to give a business presentation. "A couple of machines here can help explain how we do it." He pointed to an old wooden machine in the middle of the barn, about chest-high, which seemed to be cobbled together from several individual pieces of equipment. At the bottom of the machine was a deep, rectangular trough about six feet long. Rising up from the trough was a vertical column topped with a big, sturdy wooden funnel the size of an upside-down umbrella. On the side of the vertical column was a wooden spinning wheel that looked a bit like a captain's wheel on an old sailing ship.

"I've never seen anything like this," Holly said as she approached the machine, her eyes roving over every inch.

"It's an apple roller. Near as I can make out, it's original to the farm, probably late 1800s."

"It's been in use here ever since?"

"We believe so."

"What's it do?"

"It mills apples down to pulp, or pomace." He pointed to the funnel at the top of the roller. "After we sort and wash the apples, we load them into the funnel, a bushel at a time. When we turn the wheel, the apples are run through toothed cylinders and ground into pomace, which collects in the trough for pressing."

She bent closer to examine the trough, her curiosity increasing. "Is this how everyone mills apples?"

He shook his head. "No, there are a variety of methods. Back in England, my ancestors used a stone mill. They harnessed a horse to a big wheel set in a circular stone trough. As the horse walked the wheel around the trough, the apples in the trough got ground down."

"How does your apple roller compare?"

He shrugged. "This one's good in terms of pulp quality, but it isn't fast and it can't handle volume. During this year's harvest, we were running it nearly nonstop and still couldn't keep up. Adding a second mill is part of the plan for the coming year."

She was enjoying listening to him explain all of this. "What happens once the apples are pulped down?"

"Once we have the pomace, we press it to squeeze out as much cider as we can." He pointed toward a machine that, unlike the quaint wooden apple roller, was clearly from the industrial age. It was large and imposing, about six feet square, with heavy metal beams and gears and cylinders and pipes that rose up to the barn's rafters above. At the base of the machine was a deep, wide trough, and above the trough what looked like a huge metal press clamped down on layers of … cloth? With a puzzled frown,

Holly stepped closer. Indeed, she was looking at layers of white cloth, one atop the other.

Gabe moved to her side. "Back in the day, this hydraulic cloth press was considered state-of-the-art."

"How does it work?" she asked, running her fingers over the fabric.

"Basically, we open up the clamp, spread pomace between each layer of cloth, then press down tight."

"Kind of like making a sandwich and squeezing the heck out of it."

"Basically, yes."

"Why multiple layers of cloth?"

"Having multiple layers means we can blend in pomace from each of our three types of apples."

"A blend. Does that make the cider taste better?"

He nodded. "The Northland Orchard cider is great. It's one recipe we're really pleased with."

Holly gestured toward a shelf against the wall stacked with glass gallon jugs. "How much pomace does it take to make a gallon of cider?"

"About twelve pounds."

"Wow. And what do you do with the pomace when the juice is all squeezed out?"

"Sell it as animal feed."

She nodded, her brain whirring. "So you use the entire apple."

"That's the goal."

"How does this cloth press compare to other juice-squeezing methods?"

He shrugged. "It's not the most modern method. But it's also not our bottleneck. We might upgrade down the road, maybe in two or three years."

"One investment at a time?"

"Exactly."

"And you store the cider in...?"

"For a long time, the orchard relied almost solely on glass jugs. They transport well and are popular with folks who visit the orchard during the harvest." He pointed to the wall, which was lined with a row of gleaming stainless-steel tanks. "And now we have the tanks — our big investment this year. Increased our storage capacity four-fold."

"You mentioned storage before, when we were skating. It's important, isn't it?"

He nodded. "The better our storage, the longer our selling season."

"Does it also mean a better price?"

"It can. The main benefit is more opportunity for sales. If an opportunity arises and we have product on hand, then we can do business. But if we don't have product...."

"Then you can't."

"Exactly." He sighed, and in that moment, as worry lines creased his brow, she saw how deeply he cared about his new business and how committed he was to making it work.

"I saw the sign for the General Store next to the barn," she said.

"Our storefront. Open during the growing and harvest seasons to sell direct to the public. Want to take a look?"

"Sure."

Together, they left the barn. A gust of cold night air brushed her cheek. Across the parking area, she spied Jeremiah next to his trailer-truck, brushing Bessie's sleek flank. Through a farmhouse window, she caught movement inside.

"Who's in the farmhouse?" she asked.

"Mabel, Ike, and Ed are helping with the setup. We'll head there in a minute." He opened the door to the General Store, ushered her in, and flipped on the lights, revealing a charming retail space. It was a single room with a high vaulted ceiling and a light, airy feel — a mix of modern and rustic. A checkout counter near the entrance was well-positioned to greet customers. The walls, a soft gray-white, contrasted with the rough-hewn wood shelves lining the walls. The left side of the store appeared to be devoted to artwork and furnishings, the right side to the orchard's apple products. In the center of the space stood a huge wooden farm table, currently bare but positioned to display items.

"This is lovely," Holly said.

"Thanks. We're not stocked up, of course. That'll happen in the spring, when we open." She noted again a hint of self-consciousness in his tone, almost like he wanted her to like what she saw. Again, she got the sense that *her opinion mattered to him*....

She pointed to the farm table. "What goes there?"

"Whatever we're promoting at that moment. A couple of friends with retail experience came up from New York over the summer and helped rework the setup. What we had was good but not great, so they tweaked it. Turns out little changes can make a big difference."

"What tweaks did you make?" Holly said, her interest piqued.

"Over here, for example," he said, gesturing toward the art and furniture on the left side of the space, "when we changed our presentation of the collectibles, sales shot up."

Holly stepped closer. A selection of wooden furniture — sideboards, end tables, a chest of drawers — anchored the space. Mixed in was an assortment of vintage and handcrafted accessories — picture frames, vases, and more. A collection of antique hand lanterns stood like sentinels on one sideboard, their mix of sizes and colors and shapes pulling her in.

She noted with interest a handcrafted wine caddy, made of pine with dovetail joinery. On the caddy's door, a panoramic view of Heartsprings Lake was imprinted onto the wood. "That piece is stunning. How did the craftsman get the picture of the lake onto the wood?"

"It's a heat transfer technique," Gabe said. "You can ask Mabel about it when you meet her. She's the artist."

"Mabel, who's at the farmhouse right now?"

"Yep. She and Ike and Ed are the core team here. Can't run the orchard without them."

Her attention was drawn to a series of oil landscapes, clearly by a single hand, hanging on one wall. The scenes were rural, depicting rows of trees in the summer sun, closeups of red apples, a white clapboard farmhouse, and more.

Holly breathed in sharply as she realized what she was looking at. "Are these paintings of the orchard?"

Gabe nodded. "Ed's favorite subject."

"Ed? Ed who works here?"

"The one and same."

"Is everyone here an artist?"

He chuckled. "No. Ike and I are the un-artists here."

She cast her eye appreciatively over the collectibles area. "And your friends from New York who helped make this space sell more.... How'd they do that?"

"They made the space be what our customers want it to be."

"Meaning?"

"Most of the folks who come to the orchard are looking for more than just apples. Some are interested in the orchard experience, so for them we offer orchard tours and apple-picking days and more. Others want something tangible, something authentic, something permanent to bring back home — a memento of their trip."

"That makes sense."

"The store was already selling the work of local artists when I took on the orchard, and I knew I wanted to continue that tradition. But the artwork wasn't selling the way I thought it could and I didn't know why, so I roped in my friends and tapped their expertise."

Holly looked around. "What'd you redo?"

"The previous owners had placed the art and furniture throughout the store, which had the effect of making the art and furniture look more like decorations than collectibles. There was also too much variety. People like choices, but not too many choices."

"What's the right number of choices?"

"Three," he said without hesitation. "Four, tops. Offer five and folks get irritated and indecisive."

Holly blinked, surprised but intrigued. "So in terms of this space, it meant…."

"It meant we gathered the art and furniture together into a single gallery space. It meant we focused our selection on furniture, wall art, and vintage accessories. All by local artists. All representative of the region. In the coming year, we're expanding our social-media presence, and we'll incorporate the art into that."

Holly watched him while he talked, his passion and commitment shining through. He was being so smart about this. The smartest thing he'd done was also the hardest: Asking for help. When he realized he wasn't selling enough and didn't know how to fix that, he brought in people with the expertise to figure it out.

"How much did sales go up?"

"Tripled. Immediately."

"Wow!"

"Mabel and Ed and the other artists — they're all thrilled."

"I bet you are, too."

He nodded. "It's great. What I'm hoping is that, in time, the gallery develops a reputation, a name. If it does, it could become a reason of its own for folks to visit the orchard. The more folks we get out here, the more apple products we can sell."

"Speaking of," she said, glancing back toward the other side of the store, "what's your product lineup, exactly?"

"Apples, cider, and apple sauce. That's what the orchard has sold traditionally, and that's what we'll continue to sell. We're also looking at apple butters — the recipes I brought to the cafe — and hard ciders."

"That's five products, not three. You sure that's not too many?"

He gave her a wry smile. "No, I'm not sure at all. But it's important to try. If a new product works, that's a new revenue stream."

"And if not...."

"Then it's a mistake I add to my list and hope not to repeat."

"This is fascinating," she said, really meaning it. "And impressive." She paused, thinking about her own small business. "I'd like to get your input on what we're doing at the cafe. If little changes can make an impact...."

"To the extent I can, happy to help," he said with a grin. "Though from what I've seen, you already have a great handle on your customers and what they like."

She flushed with pleasure at the compliment. "There's always room to improve."

"You should be very proud of what you've accomplished," he said, looking directly at her. "Running a successful small business is really hard work. It takes brains and dedication and creativity and passion."

She felt her cheeks get pinker as she did her best to hold his gaze. His sincerity and intensity were impossible to shy away from. She suddenly became aware again of how tall he was and how broad his shoulders were. The air separating them seemed to crackle with energy.

Stop it, she told herself desperately. *Stop thinking like this!*

Almost as if the universe heard her plea, a car headlight chose that moment to flash through the window, reminding her that the world included more than just the two of them. A Wassail event was about to start. Involving other people.

Gabe noticed the headlights and exhaled, almost like he was taking the hint as well. He swallowed and squared his shoulders.

"Folks are arriving. How about we head to the farmhouse? That's where most of the action is."

CHAPTER 16

*T*hey made their way across the parking area toward the main house, their boots crunching lightly on the gravel, the cold night air turning their breath into fog. As they got closer, Holly's eyes wandered up over the house's white clapboard exterior, now festooned with colorful Christmas lights.

"I assume the farmhouse is where you live?" she asked.

"Yep. Home sweet home."

She followed him up the steps onto the covered porch, which wrapped around two sides of the house. It was generously deep, with comfortable chairs grouped throughout. She imagined what a wonderful place it would be to relax and enjoy the scenery during the warm summer months.

Almost as if reading her mind, Gabe pointed to a

swinging bench. "My favorite spot in the summer, after a long day out in the orchard, is right there. If I time it right, I can watch the sun slip behind the ridge and catch a few moments of quiet after a long day of work."

Holly smiled, imagining herself on that bench, rocking back and forth, the setting summer sun warming her cheeks, the air carrying hints of dry grass and freshly pressed apples.

Gabe pushed open the front door and stood aside. "After you."

Her anticipation rose as she stepped into a large, comfortable foyer with wood floors, creamy white walls, and an antique bronzed ceiling light that cast a warm glow from above. On her left, the foyer opened into the main area of the house, from which she caught the scent of fresh-baked goods. Which reminded her —

"Oh, gosh, we left the scones and chocolates in the barn."

"I'll get them. But first, let's get you settled in here."

She shrugged out of her coat, her eyes continuing to rove. A staircase rose from the foyer up to the second floor and boasted a grey carpet runner and a curved wooden banister wrapped in green tinsel. A sturdy antique oak sideboard near the front door was decorated with a potted poinsettia, its red leaves heralding the season.

After stuffing her scarf and gloves into a side pocket, she handed him her coat.

"We'll put this in the study," he said, gesturing to a room to her right. She followed him into a space that looked like it belonged to a country lawyer. The walls were lined floor to ceiling with wooden book-shelves stuffed with books. An antique oak desk and brown leather hardback chair held court on one side of the room, and a brown leather sofa and matching side chairs anchored the other. Aside from a laptop computer and a stack of papers on the desk, every-thing in the room looked like it had been there forever.

"So this is your man cave," Holly said.

Gabe chuckled. "Not really. The books are mine, but the furniture and shelves are from the previous owners. It's not exactly my taste, but the furniture is good quality, and the truth is, I haven't had time to update it."

He set Holly's coat on the sofa. "I was thinking folks could leave their stuff here when they arrive."

"Makes sense." Curious, she stepped closer to glance at his books, which appeared to be a mixture of nonfiction titles — apples, farming, small business operations — and a more diverse collection of fiction.

"You like mysteries and thrillers, I see," she said.

"Guilty as charged. Let me show you the rest of the place."

He led her back through the foyer and gestured to

the stairs. "Three bedrooms and a bathroom upstairs."

"A bathroom upstairs? Not many farmhouses from this era have that."

"The previous owners put one in about a decade ago."

"Lucky for you."

"Lucky for me."

As she stepped into the heart of the house, her eyes widened. The space was a single large room — a comfortable living area next to a dining area leading into a big kitchen. In the kitchen, a group of folks were gabbing as they loaded food onto serving trays. Christmas decorations were layered throughout. In one corner stood a big Christmas tree, its branches bursting with decorations and tinsel and lights, the star at its top nearly brushing the ceiling.

Holly turned to Gabe. "Feels very festive."

"Thanks."

"And so open."

"Thanks to the previous owners."

"They got rid of the walls —"

"And updated the kitchen, electrical, and plumbing."

"They did it in style," she said, noting the details with approval. The walls were painted the same creamy white as the foyer and the floors had the same beautiful wood — oak, she guessed. Overall, the decor was contemporary and eclectic. In this part of the house, Gabe had clearly put some effort into his furniture choices. Two facing sofas in the living area sported clean contemporary lines. A flat-screen TV hung over a brick fireplace, which was painted a crisp white to complement the softer cream of the walls. On the floor was a large area rug with the tans, golds, and greens of the natural environment.

Her gaze wandered to the teak dining table and chairs, now groaning under the weight of trays of food. "What a lovely table," she said, stepping toward it.

"Danish. Midcentury. I got it and the chairs at an estate sale."

Once again, from the way he looked at her, she sensed her opinion was of great interest to him.

From somewhere above her, she heard one of her holiday favorites — "Dance of the Sugarplum Fairy" from *The Nutcracker*. She'd always loved that ballet. She glanced up and around, looking for the stereo system. "Where are the speakers?"

Gabe pointed to the small panels in the ceiling. "Wired for sound."

"Wow."

"A nice little bonus. Especially when it's playing music I love."

"So you love *The Nutcracker,* too?"

He nodded. "Back in New York, every Christmas, my mom took me and my sister to see it."

"A family holiday tradition?"

"When I was little — four, five, six — I was into toy soldiers, so the soldiers and the giant rats were a big deal."

It took her a second before she realized what he'd just said. "Wait. The giant rats?"

"Sure. The rats that fight the soldiers."

She let out a short laugh. "I mean, you're right, but I guess when I think of the *Nutcracker*, I think about the music and the dancing...."

"And not the giant rats?"

"No," she said, laughing again.

"Well, that's what this little boy remembered." He stretched his arms wide and grinned. "Huge rats, as big as people!"

"It's funny what matters sometimes, and what sticks in your memory."

"When I got older — nine, ten — I acted like I wasn't into it anymore. Because, you know, I had gotten the idea that boys aren't supposed to like dancing and stuff like that." He shrugged. "But Mom wasn't fooled. She saw through my foot-dragging and protests and insisted every year that we go. Sure enough, the show won me over every time."

"You were so lucky to see it on stage every Christmas, in New York, on Broadway."

"Very lucky."

"Just hearing a few notes of the music is enough to remind me of Christmas. I know every piece by heart. I'll never get tired of listening to it."

"Me either," he said, his eyes on her face and seemingly happy to stay right there.

This time, she didn't shy away. "I have to tell you," she said, feeling herself being pulled closer, "I wasn't sure what to expect when I got here."

"You mean a state-of-the-art sound system wasn't what you envisioned in a century-old farmhouse?"

"Not what I envisioned at all." Really, those eyes of his were like magnets. The room was getting warmer. Maybe from the oven in the kitchen? No, the feelings of connection flowing through her were because of the handsome orchard owner at her side. The orchard owner who couldn't seem to take his eyes off of her. The orchard owner who, probably without realizing it, was leaning in, closing the distance between them....

Then she heard it — a cheerful female voice, similar to her mom's, vibrant and confident. Pulling her away from the danger zone.

"Gabriel," the voice said, from the direction of the kitchen. "Are you going to introduce us?"

CHAPTER 17

*H*olly wrenched her eyes away from Gabe's — grateful for the chance to collect herself, but immediately missing the spark between them — and turned toward the kitchen. Even with so many conflicting thoughts swirling through her, she couldn't help but note how bright and cheerful the space looked with its white cabinets, grey-white countertops, and stainless-steel appliances.

The owner of the voice, standing at the marble-topped island in the center of the kitchen, looked at her and Gabe with a gleam in her eye. She was a tall woman in her early fifties with a pleasingly round face and lovely green eyes. Her hair, short and brown and flecked with gray, seemed eminently sensible. She wore a white apron over a red sweater and, spatula in hand, was busy transferring a tray of freshly baked snickerdoodles to a serving plate.

"Mabel," Gabe said, "I'd like to introduce you to Holly."

Holly stepped forward. "Mabel, pleased to meet you."

Mabel slid the last cookie onto the plate, set the spatula down, and took Holly's hand in hers. "Holly, a pleasure."

Gabe said, "Holly owns the Heartsprings Valley Cafe on the town square."

"Oh, I've been there several times. Such a lovely place."

"Thank you," Holly said.

"Mabel and her husband Ike" — Gabe pointed to a tall, thin man who was busy unloading the dishwasher — "and Ed" — he gestured toward a short, grizzled man pouring cider at the sink — "are the core team here. The orchard can't operate without them."

Mabel stared steadily at Holly, almost as if assessing her, then nodded to herself.

To fill the pause before it became awkward, Holly said, "Gabe showed me your furniture pieces in the General Store. Consider me a fan. I love the wine caddy with the lake view imprinted on it."

"Well, thank you. Woodworking's just a little side hobby, but I enjoy it."

Gabe turned to Holly. "I'm going to get the scones

and chocolates from the barn. Okay if I leave you here?"

"Of course."

"Back in a few."

As the two women watched him walk away, Mabel sighed. "That young man works too hard."

Holly said, "He seems very committed."

"Oh, he is. But there's a rhythm to these things. Winter's supposed to be our quiet time, and Gabriel's still running a million miles an hour."

"Did you work with the previous owner as well?"

"We did. And to be frank, we weren't sure what to expect when Gabriel bought the place."

Behind her, Ike chimed in. "We weren't optimistic."

"No reason to be," Ed added.

Mabel shrugged. "A young man from New York, with no farming experience…. Let's just say we had our doubts."

"How about now?" Holly asked. "Still have doubts?"

"Oh, not me," Mabel said.

"He'll do," Ike said.

"Expect so," Ed added.

"He works hard and learns fast," Mabel said, "and keeps coming up with new ideas." She laughed. "It's tough keeping up with him sometimes — always something new!"

Holly smiled. "Like the orchard's new line of apple butters?"

Mabel's eyes brightened. "Have you tried them? What do you think?"

"He brought them to the cafe to try out, and they're delicious. I think I've found a way to add them to what we do at the cafe."

Mabel turned to Ed. "See? Our first customer."

"Looks like," Ed said.

"Ed's our voice of caution," Mabel said to Holly. "Gabriel's the one pushing us forward. Ike and I are the ones in-between."

Holly said, "Sounds like a good dynamic."

"I like how you put that." Mabel said. "Hear that, guys? We've got a good dynamic."

"Seems so," Ed said, then got back to his cider.

"Now," Mabel said, returning her full attention to Holly. "What's your story, young lady?"

Holly blinked. "My story?"

"Married? Kids? Dating? Single?"

Oh, my — so direct. Holly felt her cheeks heat up. Her immediate instinct was to deflect, to hedge, to delay, to do whatever it took to give herself a few seconds to compose a reasoned, well-considered response.

But instead, somehow, she managed to swallow, square her shoulders, and say, "No, no, no, and yes."

Mabel's face lit up. "I did that, didn't I? Asked four questions in a row?" She laughed. "Sorry for the third degree. Just wanted to get the lay of the land."

"No worries," Holly said, pleased with how she'd answered but still feeling self-conscious.

"How long have you known Gabriel?"

"Just a few days."

Ike chimed in. "He's promoting the apple butters at her cafe."

"Right," Mabel said. "Well, that explains it."

"Explains what?" Holly said.

"The lift in his step the past few days. The sparkle in his eye."

Holly blinked, the words hitting her with a jolt.

Ike said, "Either it's your cafe he likes or...."

"It's you," Ed added.

Another jolt. *Oh, my!*

Mabel, who'd been watching Holly closely, decided to take pity. "Okay, you two, enough. Let Holly be. We've got a Wassail to put on."

"Best ignore us, Holly," Ike added. "We're like this all the time. You and Gabriel are grownups. You know what's right."

"Expect so," added Ed.

Holly was about to say something — she wasn't sure what, but saying something was definitely what she planned to do — when Gabe saved the moment by returning with the scones and chocolates.

"Here we go," he said as he set the boxes on the counter. His eyes swept over them, as if sensing awkwardness and trying to suss out why. "How's everything here?"

"Great," Holly said. "Thanks for bringing those in."

"No problem."

Holly pointed to the chocolates. "Those are from Abby. For the raffle."

"And the other box?"

"That box is for testing."

"Testing?" Gabe said.

She picked up the box and turned to face him. "An apple butter taste test. Who wants to take part?"

CHAPTER 18

*I*mmediately, four pairs of very interested eyes swung toward her.

Holly smiled and cleared her throat. "At the cafe, I've been working on a new recipe for bacon scones. I've been getting close, but the recipe's been missing something. My mom suggested adding something sweet. So last night at the cafe, after everyone went home, I stayed and did some testing."

"With?" Gabe asked, intrigued.

"With your apple butters."

"Ah," he said, looking pleased and then, almost immediately, anxious. He gestured to the box. "And these are…?"

"The test samples." She opened the box, which was carefully divided into four quarters, labeled one through four. In each quarter were four bacon scones.

He leaned in and inhaled. "These smell great."

"What I did," she said, "was bake up four batches of bacon scones, each with a different Northland Orchard apple butter. And now I want your input. You and Mabel and Ike and Ed."

"Our input?" Gabe asked with surprise. "Why?"

"You have taste buds, don't you?"

"But I'm no baker."

"I'd love to know what you think," she said, then turned toward his orchard team. "All of you."

"You two get us started," Mabel said. "Have Gabriel taste first."

"Okay," Holly said. She held the box in front of him. "You ready?"

He leaned forward, still dubious. "So I should … tell you which one I like best?"

She shook her head. "Only if you like one of them the best. I want your honest reaction."

He took a deep breath. "Okay." He reached into the box. "This feels like a big deal, somehow."

Yes, it does, she agreed, even as her inner realist fought back against such nonsense. "Nope, not a big deal at all. It's just a taste test. We do this all the time."

Reassured, he picked up the first scone and chewed carefully, taking his time. "Delicious," he said.

Without having to be asked, Mabel handed Gabe a glass of water. "To cleanse your palate."

"Thanks." He took a swig, then proceeded to bite

into the second, third, and fourth scones, drinking water between each bite.

Finally, with a nod, he said, "I got it."

"Good," Holly said.

"I have a favorite. You want me to tell you?"

"In a minute. But first I want Mabel and Ed and Ike to taste as well." She handed the box of scones to Mabel, and watched as the trio quickly got down to the tastings.

"Mmm," Mabel said, her mouth full of the first scone. "You're a wonderful baker."

"Thank you."

With mounting anticipation, Holly and Gabe watched them bite into each of the test scones.

"Guys," Gabe said, "chew faster! The suspense is killing me."

Mabel laughed. "No way, no how. Some things can't be rushed."

Holly felt warmth rising on her cheeks. The way the four of them were responding to the scones was heartening. She'd always felt so blessed that her recipes brought pleasure to people.

"I have an idea," Holly said, "for how we reveal which of the four scones is your favorite. When you're all ready, put a hand behind your back, and then, at the same time, show with your fingers which scone — one, two, three or four — is your favorite."

"I like it," Gabe said.

The others apparently did, too, because it didn't

take long for them to finish chewing and put a hand behind their back. The last was Ed, who took a second bite of two scones before slowly nodding his head.

"Ready," he said.

"Okay," Holly said. "The moment of truth. Hands behind your backs. And — reveal!"

Four hands shot out. All four of them holding up — four fingers!

A rush of excitement shot through her. Careful to keep her expression neutral, she said, "It appears we have a winner." She turned to Gabe. "Why Number Four?"

Gabe took a deep breath. "All of these are delicious — each and every one — but Number Four is my favorite. I don't know if I have the vocabulary to describe what I'm tasting, but it seems the most complex. There's a richness to it, a hint of something unexpected."

For a non-baker, Holly thought, he was doing a pretty good job of explaining. "You're right about the complexity. Number Four uses your Classic apple butter — the one with the blend of three apples."

"Ah," he said.

"My mom and I both agree, by the way. Number Four is our favorite as well."

Gabe grinned. "Really?"

She grinned back. "Really."

"So what does that mean?"

"It means the cafe has a new bacon scone recipe."

His grin got bigger. "Using Northland Orchard Classic Apple Butter?"

"Yep. Which means I need to order a case, pronto."

He laughed. "Thank you for this, Holly."

"Well, you're welcome."

"I really appreciate it." His gaze intensified. Such a deep brown, those eyes of his. She felt she was being pulled closer. Like she was in a force field. Like she was caught in something that threatened to change everything. Something that promised —

She felt it then — someone reaching around her from behind and pulling her in for a friendly hug. She gasped, the physical contact returning her to reality, reminding her that she was in a busy kitchen, surrounded by people who were bustling to and fro, rushing to get everything ready for an event that would start any minute. Other folks brushed past her into the kitchen to exchange greetings with Mabel and Ed and Ike.

She heard a familiar giggle and realized the hugging arms were attached to her favorite sixteen-year-old: Amanda's younger sister Eva.

"Is that who I think it is?" Holly asked mischievously.

Eva laughed. "Merry Christmas, Holly."

Holly whipped around and pulled the girl in for a hug. She looked so much like her older sister — tall and gangly, with long blond hair pulled back into a ponytail. But unlike her serious older sister, Eva tended toward the exuberant.

"Merry Christmas, Eva. Have you met Gabe North, our host?"

Eva let Holly go, then turned and stuck out her hand. "Pleased to meet you, Mr. North. I'm Eva."

"Pleased to meet you, Eva. Call me Gabe."

"Okay, Gabe." Her wide blue eyes darted from him to Holly and then back. Then, with a grin, she turned to her sister, who was standing next to her. "You're right, Amanda. They're perfect for each other."

"Eva!" Amanda said, a flush rising on her cheeks. Gabe's eyes widened and Holly sighed, not at all surprised that the two of them had been indulging in Heartsprings Valley's favorite pastime.

"Listen, young ladies," Holly said firmly, "I'm sure Gabe can use your help before everyone arrives."

"Happy to pitch in," Amanda said, speaking equally firmly for her and her sister.

Holly turned to Gabe. "How about we have the girls help with the cider?"

"Sure," Gabe said, happy to follow Holly's lead.

Holly pointed to Ed, who was at the sink. "That's Ed. Go introduce yourselves and help him get everything set up."

"Got it," Amanda said.

Eva giggled again. "Nice to meet you, Gabe."

As she slipped by, Eva looked right at Holly and — winked!

Gabe let out a surprised laugh, and Amanda glared at her sister and pulled her away.

Once again, Holly felt her cheeks turning pink. She gestured toward the two teenagers and said, very weakly, "Kids these days."

Gabe laughed and, bless his heart, switched gears. "Look who's arrived," he said, pointing to the front door. "The mayor. I should say hi."

"Yes, go."

He headed off, giving her a chance to remind herself of an inescapable reality: Heartsprings Valley was incurably, irresistibly, insatiably meddlesome and always would be.

Another essential truth prodded her as well. Regardless of what everyone was pushing her toward, her inner realist was right: She needed to stay level-headed.

Keep things real, she told herself as she watched Gabe and the mayor from across the room. *Keep things real!*

CHAPTER 19

*T*he party really got moving then. Scores of folks arrived and filled the farmhouse with the warmth of excited conversation. After helping Mabel and Ike load cookies onto trays, Holly wandered through the gathering, exchanging greetings with friends and neighbors, most of whom she knew or recognized. Across the crowded living room, she saw her friend Becca, the town librarian, and hustled over to give her a hug, taking care to not press against the librarian's enormous belly. "So good to see you. How's everything in the baby department?"

Becca smiled and patted her belly. "Almost time. Any day now." She was a lovely woman, a few years younger than Holly, with shoulder-length brown hair and a kind, open face.

"You must be so ready."

"Oh, believe me, I am," she said with a laugh. "This little one is kicking up a storm."

"A gift of new life for Christmas."

Becca nodded, glowing. "I couldn't ask for anything more."

Holly beamed, so pleased for her and her husband Nick. Two years earlier, Becca and Nick had both been alone, both grieving lost spouses, both unwilling or unable to move forward. But now.... Holly swallowed as a wave of unexpected emotion hit her. Two years ago, Becca and Nick had found each other and together embraced life again.

"So," Becca said, her eyes wandering over the crowded room, "I hear you recently met our host."

Holly nodded. "A few days ago. He set up a table at the cafe to promote his apple products."

"Oh, I know. I've heard all about it. From, I don't know, a dozen people."

Holly couldn't help but laugh. "This town...."

Becca laughed as well. "Agree. Unbelievable."

At her side, a familiar voice said, "What's unbelievable?"

Holly turned to see Clara, who had just arrived. "Oh, you know," Holly said, giving her friend a quick hug. "This town's insane urge to meddle."

"Huh. Don't I know it." Clara's eyes widened as she took in Becca's big bump. "Girl, look at you."

Becca laughed. "You don't have to tell me."

Holly glanced around. "Clara, where's that handsome fiancé of yours?"

"Luke? Out front, doing the man talk thing with Nick and Gabe."

"About what?"

She shrugged. "A broken truck, I think."

The three women looked at each other, each thinking the same thought: *Boys and their toys.*

"I didn't know Gabe knew Nick and Luke," Holly said.

"Luke did some work out here this summer," Clara said. "I think one of the apple machines wasn't working right."

"The apple mill or the hydraulic presser?" Holly asked.

Clara looked at her with surprise. "Since when do you know the difference?"

"Since about thirty minutes ago," she replied with a shy smile.

Clara and Becca exchanged a glance and, in unison, turned their focus to Holly. They didn't say a word, instead deploying one of the most effective interrogation techniques known to humankind: silence.

Holly felt herself flush — again! — as the chasm of wordless silence lengthened. "I got here a bit early," she finally said, giving in. "Gabe gave me a tour of the place." Even as the words tumbled out, she heard how inadequate they were.

Clara cut to the chase. "You like him."

Holly saw a smile flash across Becca's face.

"I barely know him."

"It's right there in your eyes, plain as day."

"I mean," Holly stammered, "I do like him, of course. As a new neighbor and new friend. Why wouldn't I?"

Clara snorted. "Uh huh."

Becca reached out and took Holly's hands in hers. The gesture, unexpected but welcome, meant Holly had no choice but to look her friend square in the face.

Quietly and seriously, Becca said, "It's okay to be drawn to someone you just met. It can and does happen that way. Believe me, I know."

Unable to resist the force of Becca's sincerity, Holly felt herself threatening to tear up. "It scares me a little."

"Good," Becca said, giving her hands a squeeze before letting them go. "It should."

Holly blinked back a tear. She really was very lucky to know these two women. "You two are terrible. Look at me. This is all your fault."

Clara snorted again. "You're welcome."

"Okay." Becca gestured toward the front door. "Game faces, girls."

Holly turned and saw that Gabe had come back inside, along with Nick and Luke.

"Man talk done," Clara said.

Quickly, Holly arranged her mouth into a smile. Luke and Nick strode toward them, followed by Gabe, and soon all six were swept up in conversation. As even more folks arrived, the warmth and joy of the season seemed to spread. At a certain point her mom and dad joined them, and soon after, George and his wife Millie.

With the party ebbing and flowing around her, Holly found herself with a cup of wassail in her hand and Gabe at her side. The wassail, served in a clear glass mug with a cinnamon stick, was toasty-warm to the touch and smelled wonderfully of apples and spices.

"I don't even know how this ended up in my hands," she said, bringing the mug to her nose to breathe in its aroma.

"I put it there, a few seconds ago," Gabe said.

She inhaled again. "Let me guess what's in it."

"Go for it."

"Heated cider, with eggs mixed in."

He nodded.

"Along with roasted apples, sugar, nutmeg...."

"Yep."

"Ginger...."

"Yep."

"And what else?"

"Cloves."

"Ah."

She swirled the cinnamon stick in the wassail and

took a sip, enjoying the drink's heat and taste. "It's lovely."

"Thanks."

"Old family recipe?"

He grinned. "Found a bunch of recipes on the Internet, tried them all, and went with the best one."

She chuckled. "Well, you picked well." She took another sip. "I still don't really know what a Wassail event is."

He glanced at his watch. "In about five minutes, you get to find out. Could I ask for your help? In a minute or two, could you help herd folks to the back porch?"

"Sure thing."

"See you in a few."

She watched him make a beeline for Mabel and Ike and then the mayor. A minute later, Mabel rang a bell and said, over the hubbub of the crowd, "Everyone, please make your way out back."

The curious crowd murmured to each other as they stepped out onto the farmhouse's back deck. Strung with lights, the deck overlooked a grand old apple tree in the backyard. Holly smiled when she saw a big, sturdy apple stand positioned next to the tree, with "Merry Christmas" spelled out in green apples against a background of red apples.

Gabe and the mayor stepped down onto the snow-covered ground in front of the tree, and Gabe turned to address the crowd. "Everyone, Merry

Christmas and welcome to Northland Orchard."
After the crowd applauded, he continued. "Thank
you for joining us here tonight. All of us here at the
orchard — Mabel and Ike and Ed and I — are
grateful you've joined us for what we hope will
become an annual holiday event."

Mabel, carrying a beautiful silver bowl filled with
apple cider, joined Gabe and the mayor in front of the
tree.

"Wassailing," Gabe continued, "is an old English
tradition dating back centuries. The belief was that
singing to the apple trees and pouring cider on their
roots would encourage a bountiful harvest in the
coming year. My English ancestors, who owned
orchards south of London in the 1800s, held Wassails
of their own."

The crowd murmured with interest, and Gabe
continued. "Now, as a modern kind of guy, I'm not
necessarily sold on the idea that singing to trees will
produce more apples." The crowd chuckled. "But, as
a modern kind of guy, I'm certainly willing to give it
a shot. As a new friend just reminded me" — his eyes
scanned the porch and landed on Holly — "trying
new things can lead to wonderful results."

Holly blinked, pleased and surprised. Next to her,
Clara nudged her.

"Quiet," Holly whispered.

"I didn't say anything," Clara whispered right
back.

Gabe resumed. "With the help of the Internet" — more chuckles — "I found a wassailing poem that I'd like to recite tonight here in front of this big old apple tree, which we believe is the oldest on the farm. I like to imagine that my ancestors, two centuries ago, did something similar back in merry old England." He pulled out a sheet of paper from his coat pocket and said, his voice full of energy:

Apple tree, apple tree, we all come to wassail thee,
Bear this year and next year to bloom and to blow,
Hat fulls, cap fulls, three cornered sack fills,
Hip, Hip, Hip, hurrah!
Holler biys, holler hurrah!

The crowd, caught up in the moment, joined Gabe in the final hearty *hurrah*, then burst into applause.

Gabe said, "I think the tree wants to hear some Christmas carols!" He turned to the mayor. "What do you say, Mr. Mayor?"

The mayor nodded and launched into a spirited rendition of "Jingle Bells." Within seconds, everyone was joining in. As the familiar words rose up into the night sky, Mabel passed the bowl to Gabe, and Gabe carefully poured the cider over the big tree's roots.

As the song ended, the crowd applauded again, clearly pleased with this new tradition. "One last thing before we head back inside," Gabe said. "I know the mayor wants to update us on the Heart-springs Valley Christmas charity drive."

The mayor stepped forward. "Thank you, every-one, for your generosity this season and for opening your hearts and wallets to support our veterans and their families. We set a very ambitious goal this year, and I'm pleased to announce we've come very, very close to reaching it."

Holly felt her stomach clench. She'd been expecting this result — close but not quite there — for a couple of weeks. But it was still hard to hear the words spoken. The mayor, despite his brave face, had to be disappointed.

"Now," the mayor said, "I know you're all eager to hear who won the raffle prizes. With the help of the lovely Mabel, let's pick some winners!"

As he and Mabel pulled the winning tickets from a jar, Holly found herself slipping through the crowd to Amanda and George and whispering a question in their ears. When they both smiled and nodded, Holly scooted over to her mom and whispered the same. When her mom's face lit up, Holly made her way to the front of the crowd. After the mayor announced the final winning ticket, Holly cleared her throat and said, loudly enough to be heard, "Bert? Mayor Winters?"

Bert looked across the crowd until he found her. "Yes, Holly?"

With a voice that thankfully sounded clear and

confident, she said, "Since we're so close to our goal with our charity drive, the team at Heartsprings Valley Cafe would love to get us across the finish line. George and Amanda and my mom and I are happy to announce a new fund-raiser."

"A new fund-raiser?" Bert echoed, his eyes lighting up.

"Tomorrow evening, at the Heartsprings Valley Cafe, we'd like to invite everyone to an old-fashioned Christmas ice-cream social."

Her mom stepped up next to her and exclaimed, "Everyone, we're throwing a party!"

The crowd laughed and applauded.

"The proceeds will benefit the Christmas drive," Holly said, "so please plan on attending. Tomorrow night, starting at eight!"

CHAPTER 20

*O*h, dear.

What had she done?

What manner of irrational exuberance had over-taken her?

What unstoppable events had she set in motion?

A full day had passed — a nearly sleepless night, to be specific, along with a crazy-busy morning and an even busier afternoon — since her impulsive offer. She'd barely had time to breathe as she and her team rushed to and fro, trying to cram the hundreds of tasks required for a big event into a few hours of concentrated activity.

It was now early evening. The last of the cafe's regular customers had left a few moments earlier. She stood in the front room, running an expert gaze over the space, looking for the next item that needed tackling, trying to keep an even throttle on the mix of anticipation and adrenaline charging through her. In one short hour, the cafe would reopen. Given Heart-springs Valley's love of ice cream, she expected a big crowd.

And still so much to do! Hosting an event was *work*. And to do it all at the last minute, without any planning, riding on emotion and optimism, during the cafe's busiest season — what in the world had she been thinking? Clearly, her inner rationalist had taken a holiday.

At the thought of the extra effort she was asking of her mom and Amanda and George, she felt a pang of guilt. Still, she reminded herself, she'd asked them before committing, and they'd all agreed to do it. In fact, based on how they were bustling about now, they actually seemed quite keen, working together effortlessly to get things ready.

A welcome feeling — of gratitude — flowed through her, strong enough that she had to swallow back the emotional surge. Yes, the ice-cream social was a good thing to be doing. The mayor, of course, had been thrilled. Reaching the fundraising goal was important to him, especially given the cause. He'd been out all day, spreading the word and rallying folks to attend.

And Gabe — well, there was no other way to put it: He'd been terrific. He'd been at the cafe all after-noon, pitching in to make sure everything was ready, turning himself into a one-man delivery service, running to get ice cream and extra supplies and so much more. At this particular moment, he was a furniture-moving machine. Over the past few minutes, at Holly's request, he'd carried half of the front room's tables and chairs into the back. Now he stood in the center of the front room, positioning the long table that would act as ice-cream serving station.

"Yes, a little more to the right," she said. Carefully, he inched the table over. "Good. Tablecloth's in the pantry."

"Got it," he said. "What next?"

He seemed so attentive as he looked at her, waiting for direction. So eager and upbeat. Like he was enjoying himself. Like he was happy to pitch in. He was dressed in the same practical getup — boots, jeans, red plaid shirt — he wore most days. Her eyes paused on his shirt, recalling the crisp blue collared number he'd sported a few days earlier. A shame he wouldn't have time to change into that. The blue in that shirt had worked well with his brown hair and eyes....

She realized the silence had gone on longer than expected. Gabe's brow was furrowed, like he was puzzled. Then, to her surprise and dismay, he glanced down at his shirt. Had he seen her staring at it? Was she *that completely obvious*?

Apparently she was, because the next thing out of his mouth was, "By the way, I brought a change of clothes. They're in my truck."

She swallowed. "I'm sorry, I didn't mean to suggest...."

He grinned. "Hey, no worries. I know how parties work."

"You've been fantastic today — I can't thank you enough."

He shook his head. "After everything you've done for the orchard the past week, it's the least I can do." His gaze became intense again, even serious. Like he was full of emotion inside, straining to burst forth.

She blinked, the fluttering in her stomach a reminder of all the unreasonable ideas that this man seemed capable of sparking within her. "Well, I appreciate it." She glanced at the clock on the wall and gasped. "Oh, gosh."

"I know. Clock's a-ticking. What do you want me to do next?"

"Let's arrange the remaining tables and chairs along the sides. Most folks will stand and mingle, but some will want to sit."

"Tablecloths for them?"

"Also in the pantry."

Her mom hustled out of the kitchen and said, "Holly, can you go talk to George? He has a question about the scones."

"Sure. Can you help Gabe with the setup?"

Her mom nodded, Holly headed into the kitchen, and before she knew it, they were all caught up in the rush of preparation. All too soon, the clock was telling her it was time to play hostess. Quickly, she stepped into the tiny bathroom in the back of the cafe and changed into her pink silk blouse and slimming black slacks. She paused briefly in front of the tiny mirror. There was nothing she could do about her hair now — it was what it was. And it was ... *fine*, she acknowledged. Not great, not terrible. Just ... *normal*. Normal, brown, shoulder-length hair, washed and shampooed that morning. She sighed, for just a second lost in thought....

A knock at the door startled her.

"Out in a sec!" Holly said.

"No rush," Amanda said. "Just wanted to make sure you were in there."

"Everything okay?"

"Fine. Folks are starting to arrive."

Holly turned back to the mirror and gave her face a hasty final once-over. Eyes, fine. Cheeks, fine. Lips — not fine. Quickly, she applied gloss, gave herself a "you can do it, girl" look, squared her shoulders, left the bathroom, and made her way toward the hubbub of conversation already emanating from the front room.

Hostess time!

CHAPTER 21

$\mathcal{T}$o no one's surprise, the ice-cream social quickly became packed. Laughter and conversation flowed as the cafe filled with happy faces. Bert had encouraged folks to wear their most Christmassy sweaters, and scads of folks had done just that. Everywhere she looked, Holly saw sweaters bedecked with reindeer, snowmen, Santa, elves, Christmas trees, and so much more.

Gabe appeared at her side, looking fresh and pressed in his crisp pale-blue collared shirt and dark slacks.

"Where's your over-the-top Christmas sweater?" she asked.

He smiled. "Next year."

Looking around, she saw nothing that required her immediate attention. Now was as good a time as any for what she'd been planning all day. "I want to show you something," she said, gesturing for him to follow.

"Show me what?" he asked, curiosity in his tone.

She led him to the counter, where she picked up her recipe folder and opened it.

"A new addition to the cookbook?" he said, looking over her shoulder.

She nodded. "The bacon scones, with their star ingredient." She ran her fingers down the recipe ingredients to the newest one: Northland Orchard Classic Apple Butter.

"Wow," he said. "Love it."

She looked up at him and was touched by the sincerity in his eyes.

His gaze intensified. "Can't tell you how much this means."

She swallowed back a flutter of excitement and steeled herself for her next step. "But wait, there's more."

"More?" he repeated, eyebrows rising.

With a hand that she somehow managed to keep steady, she flipped a few pages to the two-page spread for her cranberry-apple scone — her cafe's signature item. It was the first recipe she'd perfected, the item that continued to outsell everything else on her menu, the treat that had given her the confidence to dream big and take a leap and open her cafe. On the left side of the two-page spread was the scone's recipe, and on the right, a blank spot.

"This is your cafe's top scone," he said.

"That's right."

"Your best-seller."

"That's right."

"But this recipe is already perfect."

"Almost," she said. "Something's missing."

"What's missing?"

"Its pairing. Its partner. Its perfect match."

Gabe went still. "What are you saying?"

"What I'm saying," Holly said, doing her best to keep her voice steady, "is that I've found it." She reached into her pocket and took out a piece of paper, folded into quarters. "If you'll do the honors."

With a questioning look, Gabe took the paper, unfolded it, and breathed in sharply. "Is this what I think it is?"

"Yes."

He scanned the paper again, then aimed his deep brown eyes at her. "My wassail recipe?"

"Yes."

"It's the match for your scone?"

"Yes."

"How do you know?"

"I brought some back to the cafe last night and did another taste test."

"And you found…."

"It goes perfectly with the scone."

"For real?" he said, blinking suddenly, as if battling back tears.

"Yes," she said, feeling her eyes coming close to tearing up as well. "For real."

For a long second, as they looked into each other's eyes, she felt herself calming. The connection, the spark, that had been there from the first really was there, and now it was grounded in something new — an awareness, shared by them both, that what was happening was good and right and true.

Gabe cleared his throat. "Holly, I'd like to ask you something."

She felt her heart flutter with anticipation. "Yes, Gabe?"

He swallowed. "I'd like to —"

Before he could finish, a familiar voice intruded with, "Holly! Great news!"

Wait. What?

Holly turned.

Mayor Winters was standing there, right next to her, a huge smile on his face.

Your timing is terrible, she wanted to say. Instead, she took a deep breath. "What news, Bert?"

He let out a big laugh and pulled her in for a quick hug. "We did it, thanks to you!"

"Did what?"

The mayor laughed again and picked up a glass, tapped it with a spoon, and announced to the room, in a booming, hearty voice, "Everyone, if I could have your attention for just a moment!"

It took a few seconds, but the crowd hit the pause

buttons on their conversations and turned to the mayor.

"Thank you," the mayor said. "Thank you all so much. I have wonderful news. Due to your incredible generosity, we've hit the goal for the Christmas charity drive!" The room erupted in cheers and applause. After waiting for the noise to subside, the mayor added, "A huge thanks to all of the local businesses who pitched in to make this happen, including Holly and the terrific team here at Heartsprings Valley Cafe."

More applause followed, and eyes turned toward Holly, who realized she was expected to say something. "George and Amanda and my mom and I are so happy to help out for such a worthy cause," she said to the crowd.

"Three cheers for Holly," the mayor said. "Hip hip, hurray!" The crowd joined in with, "Hip hip, hurray! Hip hip, hurray!"

Holly's cheeks flushed with embarrassment and pleasure. She bit her lip to hold back the wave of emotion.

"Now, back to the party," the mayor said. "Merry Christmas!"

Her mom rushed to her side and pulled her in for a hug. "You did good, dear."

"*We* did good," Holly said, returning the hug and trying to keep her voice even and her eyes moisture-free. "I couldn't have done it without you."

Her mom gave her another squeeze and laughed. "And don't you forget it!"

Gabe said, "Look at the two of you."

"Two of a kind? Peas in a pod?" her mom joked.

"A wonderful pair," he said, his eyes landing on Holly and staying there.

Holly swallowed. "Well, you deserve thanks, too. We couldn't have pulled this off without you."

"Amen," her mom threw in. She disengaged from Holly and pointed to the recipe folder. "I saw you two talking about this from across the room. What's up?"

Holly and Gabe glanced at each other, and then Holly said, "You tell her."

"You sure?"

"Absolutely."

Gabe opened the folder to the cranberry-apple scone recipe and started explaining, her mom uttering some very pleased oohs and aahs.

Later on, when Holly thought back on that moment, she recognized it as the instant before everything changed. Out of the corner of her eye, she noticed the cafe door swing open and Mabel step in with a tall, beautiful woman. The woman said something to Mabel and started scanning the crowd. The woman was in her early thirties, with an elegant face and long brown hair, and looked effortlessly chic in a coat of rich caramel wool with a festive red silk scarf. She wasn't from around here — Holly was sure of that. Perhaps she was a friend or relative of Mabel's, visiting for the holidays?

Somewhat anxiously, the woman's expressive eyes roved over the room, as if she were looking for someone in particular.

Then the eyes stopping roving. And Holly stopped breathing.

The woman was walking toward her.

No, not toward her.

Toward *Gabe*.

He hadn't seen the woman yet — his back was toward her — and right now he was laughing merrily at something her mom had just said.

Holly realized she hadn't heard what her mom had just said. Why was that? Why hadn't she been paying attention? Surely the beautiful woman with the lovely eyes slipping through the crowd had nothing to do with her sudden lack of focus? After all, why would she be the reason she couldn't concentrate on a simple conversation? The woman was a stranger, after all. A friend or relative of Mabel's. There was no reason for her arrival to be cause for distraction. No reason at all.

Yet the knot forming in Holly's stomach disagreed.

Before she could ask her stomach what was up, the woman reached Gabe. For a split second, indecision and uncertainty flashed across the woman's face, then vanished as she took a deep breath and tapped Gabe on the shoulder.

Gabe felt the tap and turned.

And blinked.

His mouth fell open. His face drained of color. His back stiffened.

After several seconds that seemed go on forever, he said, voice hoarse with surprise, "Carrie? What are you doing here?"

All at once, the room seemed to fade into the background. Her mom inhaled sharply.

Gabe shot a startled glance at Mabel, who, clearly uncomfortable, said, "She pulled into the orchard as I was getting ready to head out, and asked where you were. I told her you'd be back later, but she wanted to join you and asked if I could drive her here...."

Gabe turned back to Carrie. "What are you doing here?"

Carrie said, "I drove up to see you."

"To see me," he repeated, clearly stunned.

"Yes," Carrie said. She paused for a second, as if choosing a course of action, then arranged a smile on her face and turned to Holly and her mom. "But first, please, introduce me to your friends."

Gabe's mouth opened, then closed. His eyes shot to Holly, as if pleading with her. But pleading for what? Help? Understanding?

Forgiveness?

Holly's mom stepped into the breach. "I'm Bev,"

she said to Carrie, then gestured to Holly. "And this is my daughter Holly, the owner of this cafe."

"Pleased to meet you both," Carrie said, looking around brightly. "You have such a beautiful place. It smells so wonderful in here."

"Thank you," Bev said. "And you are…?"

"Oh, I'm sorry. I'm Carrie. I'm a … friend of Gabe's." She paused, then added, "From New York."

The New York part was unnecessary, of course. As was the fact that she was a lot more than a friend. The stunned look on Gabe's face spoke volumes.

Holly swallowed and took a deep breath. A familiar painful weight was settling into the pit of her stomach. A weight she knew all too well. A weight that was clearly her fate, her burden, to bear as she moved through this life.

As had happened before, her inner realist stepped up to earn its keep and do what needed doing. She heard herself say, in a steady voice, "Carrie, nice to meet you." And then, the real question: "What brings you to Heartsprings Valley?"

After a pause that went on at least a second too long, Carrie said, "I came up to see Gabe." Her eyes swung to him. "To … talk."

"Talk?" he repeated, still flummoxed.

"About…." She looked around. "Would it be all right if we went someplace more private?"

Gabe blinked, seemingly unable to speak.

"Would that be all right?" Carrie repeated.

Gabe exhaled, then nodded. "Of course." The decision seemed to settle him. He turned toward Holly, his gaze filled with concern. "I need to go."

"I know," Holly said, her voice somehow still steady.

"I'm sorry. I'll...." He paused, then said, "I'll see you soon."

"Of course. Thank you again for your help today."

With reluctance, Gabe allowed Carrie to lead him away.

Silently, the three women watched the two of them leave the cafe and vanish into the night.

Her mom slowly turned to Mabel. "Is that his ex-girlfriend?"

Mabel nodded.

"The one he broke up with?"

Mabel nodded again.

"And she's here because?"

Mabel sighed. "She wants him back." Her eyes shot to Holly. "I'm sorry."

Very briskly, Holly said, "There's nothing to be sorry about."

A total lie. A lie which fooled no one. Though maybe, if she repeated it over and over, she'd start believing it herself.

She took a deep breath. She had things to do. A party to run. People to greet. Tasks to complete. So much to do. Yes, so much to do! She turned to Mabel.

"Now that you're here, please be sure to have some ice cream. Mom, maybe you can help her?"

She felt her lips starting to tremble — always a warning sign. Tasks — yes, tasks to do. "I have stuff to do in the back. If you'll excuse me?"

Stiffly, she fled into the kitchen. At the grill, George looked over his shoulder. "What do you need, boss?"

"Nothing." Another lie.

He looked back again, as if he'd noticed something. "What's going on?"

"Nothing."

His eyes narrowed. "What'd he do?"

"Nothing."

"He out there right now?"

"He left."

"Why?"

She took a deep breath. Tasks weren't going to help. She had to get out of here before she dissolved, before she collapsed, while she still possessed a modicum, a shred, of self-control. She walked across the kitchen to the coat rack and threw on her scarf and coat. "George, can you tell Amanda and Mom I'm not feeling well? I'm sorry to rush out, but I should get home."

He frowned. "Go. We'll be fine. Go."

"Thank you." With that, she stepped out the back door, tears streaming down her face, and rushed out into the night.

CHAPTER 22

*H*olly became aware of morning light filtering through her bedroom curtains. As the terrible events of the previous night came roaring back, she burrowed her head beneath her blankets and groaned.

What a fool she'd been. To actually believe that maybe, just maybe, she and Gabe had a chance. How unrealistic to believe they might someday….

She curled up tighter. Her whole body ached, and not just from the strains of rushing to prepare the cafe for the ice-cream social. The prospect of getting out of bed today was laughable. How many times in her life had she allowed herself to believe in the possibility of love, only to have that possibility dashed? *All of those times*, that was how many. Every single one of those times, without exception.

Including this one. Tears threatened. With a rush of

anger, she battled them back. This time seemed to hurt so much more. She and Gabe — they'd had a real connection. The pull she felt seemed so right. How naive she'd been to believe they actually stood a chance.

His ex was quite pretty, she forced herself to acknowledge. Taller than her, slimmer than her, younger than her…. It was fate, of course, that she showed up right before Christmas…. To tell him she'd made a huge mistake and wanted to get back together, and was ready to live her life with him, together forever. The shock on his face had been unmistakable, along with the apologetic look in his eyes as his ex took him by the hand and led him away….

Holly coughed to stifle a sob. She couldn't face the world — not today. But she'd have to call the cafe. They'd be wondering where she was. She reached out from beneath the covers, grabbed the phone on her night table, turned it on, and cracked an eyelid as it powered up. Two voicemails — both from Gabe. Pain stabbed through her. No, she couldn't deal with what he was going to say. Didn't want to hear it. Couldn't bear the sound of his voice telling her that he and his ex were getting back together. No way, no how, no dice. Tomorrow maybe, when she was stronger. But not today.

She called the cafe. Amanda picked up on the first ring.

"Holly, where are you? Are you heading in? We were starting to get worried."

"I'm sorry, Amanda, but I woke up this morning feeling terrible." She coughed, somewhat unconvincingly, and continued. "I think I'm coming down with something, so I'm going to have to take a sick day."

"Oh, gosh, I'm sorry to hear that. Can we bring you anything?"

"No, no, no," she said immediately, wanting nothing of the sort. Interaction with another human being, especially a human who understood the meaning of the previous night's events, was the last thing she needed. Sympathy, especially right now, would be too painful. "I'm good here. All set."

"You sure?"

"Positive. My plan today is to turn off my phone and sleep this off."

"Okay," Amanda said, sounding unsure. "I'll let George and Bev know."

At the thought of what her absence would mean — four days before Christmas, the cafe jammed with folks placing last-minute orders — she almost changed her mind. "You know, if I get up and moving, I think I'll be able to —"

"No," Amanda said firmly. "No, you're staying home today. This is me making a management decision, boss. I'll call my sister and have her come in to help with the rush. You're not feeling well and you need to get better, and we simply can't have you here. You'll get us all sick and we can't have that."

Holly smiled at the confidence in her protégé's voice. "If you say so."

"Good," Amanda said. "Then that's settled."

"I'm sorry about this," Holly said, already regretting what she'd set in motion.

"You get better, boss. We're good here. Get some sleep, okay?"

"Okay."

"I want you to do what you said you'd do — turn off your phone and get some sleep."

"Got it."

"Hope you feel better soon."

"Thank you."

With a click, Amanda was gone, off to manage a busy day made even busier by Holly's absence. Another pang of guilt rippled through her, subsiding only when she allowed other thoughts in. She'd worked so hard for so long. A day off wasn't the end of the world. Amanda was ready for the challenge. Tomorrow would be here soon enough.

With a deep sigh, she pressed the "off" button on the phone, burrowed deeper under her blanket, and slipped into fitful slumber.

CHAPTER 23

She felt herself being yanked out of dreamless sleep by an insistent banging sound.

The source of which, she surmised from deep beneath her covers, was someone pounding … on her front door? Reluctantly, she cracked her eyelids open and slid the covers from her face. Sunlight was no longer pouring through her curtains. Which meant … it was night?

Had she slept all day?

She struggled upright, gasping as her spine cracked with the sudden movement. Groaning, she clambered out of bed, stepped to the window, and pulled back the curtain. Yes, it was dark outside. The door-pounding from below ceased and a familiar figure, bundled up against the cold, stepped back from the front porch and stared up at her bedroom window.

"Holly Ann Snow!" her mom yelled as she caught sight of her. "You open this door right now!"

"Sorry," Holly mumbled.

She let the curtain drop and hurried downstairs, still clad in the loose sweats, baggy t-shirt, and wool socks she'd gone to bed in, and opened the door. Cold air rushed in, effortlessly penetrating the wool covering her toes. Her mom stood there for a second, clearly annoyed, then stepped in. "I was beginning to get worried. Why didn't you answer?"

"I was asleep."

"Asleep? You slept *all day*?"

"Didn't Amanda tell you? I wasn't feeling well."

Her mom shot her a skeptical glance, then began unbuttoning her coat. "Look at you. You're a mess. We need to get you cleaned up."

"Mom, I'm fine."

"No, you're not." Her mom paused unbuttoning to give her daughter her full attention. "And I know why, dear, but now is not the time to go into that. We need to get you to the cafe — pronto — and you need to look nice."

"Why?"

"The state fire inspector, that's why! We've been calling *all afternoon*. He showed up for a surprise inspection and needs to talk with you right away about the results."

"Wait, what?" Holly moved toward the coat rack. "We can go right now —"

"No, no, no!" her mom said, intercepting her. "Not a chance. You need to look like a professional, not like you just rolled out of bed, which is apparently what you just did. Do you want to come across as a slob, or as a responsible businesswoman? Amanda and George are keeping the inspector busy right now, which means if you hurry through a shower, we can get you presentable."

"Mom—"

"Don't you 'Mom' me. This is an order. Scoot!"

There was no arguing with her mom when she was like this, and besides, her reasoning was sound, so Holly allowed herself to be pushed into the shower. A few minutes later, wrapped in her terry-cloth bathrobe, she sat on the edge of her bed and watched her mother rifle through her closet for the right outfit.

"What did the inspector say?"

"Something about vents and exhaust fans, dear, I don't know." She handed Holly a pair of black tights to slip on, then pulled out one of Holly's favorite dresses — a simple yet elegant dark-blue silk dress, knee-length with long sleeves. "This will work."

Holly slipped into the tights. "Mom —"

"No arguments, young lady. Arms above your head."

As Holly allowed her mom to help her into the

dress, she realized that having her mom there was so
… reassuring. Having her fuss over her was nice.
Very nice. More than that — it was important. It
meant the world to have her here. How blessed she
was to have this wonderful woman — this upbeat,
peppy woman who sometimes drove her a bit batty
— as her mom.

Holly swallowed back a surge of emotion. "You're
always here to look out for me, aren't you?"

"Of course, dear. Always."

"Thank you. I love you, Mom."

"I love you, too, dear," her mom said, focused on
the dress. "Now stop distracting me. Straighten your
posture so I can zip you up." She turned her around
and examined her critically. "Yes, this will do. Now
your face."

"Mom —"

"Quiet, young lady." She guided Holly to the bed,
sat her down, zipped into the bathroom, returned
with foundation and eyeliner and blush, and got to
work.

"All this for a fire inspector?"

"No, for your *future*. You've put so much into the
cafe. This is for *you*."

"Mom," Holly said, feeling her eyes start to tear
up, "I'm sorry about today. I should have been
stronger. I shouldn't have played hooky."

"Shush." Her mom started applying blush, her
movements deft and assured. "We'll talk about that

later. One thing at a time. First things first. And don't you dare start crying — you'll ruin your face."

It was a relief to hear her mom acknowledge what had happened the previous night, and even more of a relief not to have to talk about it. She might be ready to go there tomorrow — but not today. It was so comforting simply to have her mom there with her, expressing her sympathy and love through the careful application of makeup.

After a few minutes of brushing and lining, her mom stepped back and nodded. "Okay, you're fine now."

"Just fine?"

"Very pretty. And professional. You should do this more often."

Together, they made their way downstairs. Holly sat down on the bench to get into her boots.

"No, no, no," her mom said, handing her her favorite pair of black heels.

"Really?" Holly said. "You remember it's winter outside."

"I'll make sure you don't slip. It's only a short walk."

With a sigh, Holly again accepted the inevitable. "I can't see how a pair of heels will make a difference."

"The extra height, dear. You never know. Come on, let's get a move on."

They donned their winter coats, wrapped scarves

around their necks, and slipped on their winter gloves. "Okay," Holly said, "let's go." She followed her mom out into the cold night air. The sky overhead was clear, the stars bright through the branches of the bare trees.

Her mom slipped her arm through hers and led her down the walkway to the sidewalk, then aimed them toward the town square for the five-minute walk to the cafe. Together, in companionable silence, they made their way past neighbors' homes decorated with snowmen and reindeer and colored lights galore.

"I'm very proud of you, you know," her mom said.

"Thank you."

"I worry I don't say that enough."

"Nothing to worry about on that score."

"Well, I do worry," her mom said, guiding them past an icy patch on the sidewalk. "So let me just say this now. I have so much respect for the decisions you've made and the woman you've become — for the hard work and long hours, the sweat and dedication, the care and attention and *love* you show others every single day."

Aww.... Holly felt more tears sneaking up. "Thank you."

"You've made so many good and right choices with the cafe. You have a wonderful team there with George and Amanda —"

"And of course you."

"— and me. The people of this town love your cafe, and they love you."

"Mom," she said, finding it necessary again to blink back tears.

"Shush, dear. Right now, I need you to listen to your mother."

They'd reached the town square, the heart of Heartsprings Valley. After looking both ways, her mom led her across the street into the square. Soft white lights lined the path, illuminating the army of snowpeople decorating the snow-covered ground. Crisp air flowed over her legs, reminding her that a fire inspector was awaiting her — an inspector who needed to discuss inspection results that sounded ominous. It was a sign of how out-of-sorts she was — how unfocused and distracted she was — that the impending meeting wasn't worrying her more. Normally, her mind would be racing, trying to antici- pate and prepare for what she'd soon be told....

"What I need to say," her mom said, interrupting her train of thought, "is that you deserve all the happiness in the world. And all of us feel that way."

"Mom, thank you, but I —"

"I'm not done, dear." They'd crossed the square and were now across the street from the cafe, the familiar wooden cafe sign standing proudly over the front door. Through the big windows, Holly saw that the lights were dimmed, except for what looked like a single light at one table.

She blinked when she saw the light flicker. Like a candle would. An odd lighting choice for a meeting with a fire inspector.

Her mom, her arm still entwined in hers, led her across the street. Holly peered through the window when they reached the cafe's front door. Yes, she'd been right. The light was a *candle*. What was going on?

Her mom turned her toward her. "Darling, you deserve to be happy. So get in there and grab the brass ring. Seize your moment. Embrace your future."

"Mom —"

"I love you, dear." Her mom pulled her in for a tight hug, then stepped back, her eyes glistening. "Now stop dawdling and scoot."

"Mom…," she said, her voice trailing off as she realized, with a jolt, that all was *not* as advertised.

"Inside — now." With a final loving glance, her mom turned and slipped away into the night.

CHAPTER 24

*H*er heart figured it out before the rest of her did. Her brain was still trailing far behind, still fogged with confusion, even as the organ in the center of her chest started thumping away, uncontrollable and untamable. Her cheeks flushed pink. For a long second, she felt faint, even a bit light-headed.

What was going on? Could this be…?

With a trembling hand, she pushed open the door of her cafe and stepped inside. Heat rushed over her, along with the wonderful aromas of freshly baked treats. Music played softly in the air.

Amanda appeared from behind the counter, dressed like a maître d' in a crisp white button-down shirt and black slacks. With a smile, she helped Holly out of her coat. "If you'll follow me," she said.

A million questions raced through Holly's head,

but not a single one managed to make it to her lips. Wordlessly, she allowed her protégé to lead her to the candle-lit table, covered in a crisp white tablecloth, in the center of the cafe.

George, dressed in white and black as well, appeared with two champagne flutes and a bottle of bubbly in an ice bucket, which he set on the table.

Amanda reached in and gave her a hug. In George's eyes, Holly could have sworn she saw tears.

"What are you two up to?" she whispered, still not ready to believe, but desperately wanting to.

"Good luck, boss," George said.

"Go get him," Amanda whispered.

As Amanda broke the hug and stepped away, Holly's gaze wandered past her and landed on —

Gabe.

He'd stepped out from the back and now stood before her in a dark suit and tie, dashing and gorgeous, a single red rose in his hand, his eyes locked on her. He seemed so serious, so alert, so intense, his attention and energy — his every fiber — focused on one thing:

Her.

She couldn't help herself — she gasped. Without hesitation, he strode toward her and swept her into his arms.

"What's going on?" she managed to say, her heart racing as he pulled her in tight. He felt so strong holding her, so solid. She caught a hint of his aftershave, and his confidence thrilled and reassured her.

He leaned in, his lips brushing her ear. "I realized I haven't been wooing you properly," he murmured. "I needed to address that oversight, pronto."

His arms felt wonderful around her. His cheek — warm and freshly shaved – nuzzled hers. Behind her, she sensed George and Amanda setting plates and silverware and a tray of treats on the table.

The music, she realized, was "Waltz of the Flowers" from *The Nutcracker*.

He took a step back and extended his hand. "Shall we dance?"

Blinking back tears, she saw longing and hope in his eyes.

"I'd love that," she said.

With the same confidence and grace he'd displayed on the ice, he took her in his arms and led her around the room. She felt herself relaxing in the flow of movement, her body in tune with his, the music carrying them effortlessly, the lovely, familiar rhythms of the waltz guiding them across the floor. Out of the corner of her eye, she saw George and Amanda put on their winter coats and slip out the front door, leaving the cafe to her and Gabe.

It felt like a dream. A wonderful dream. As the music came to a close, she felt herself floating, ever so gently, back to earth. For a long moment, arms still entwined, they stood silent, gazing into each other's eyes.

Slowly, she exhaled. She had to know. Even if it meant breaking the spell. Standing straighter, working up the courage, she said, "What about … Carrie?"

He took a step back, his hands finding hers so he could face her directly. "Carrie has returned to New York, where she belongs," he said, his eyes not leaving hers, his tone serious, even somber. "She asked me to take her back. I told her no." He swallowed back a surge of emotion, then continued. "I'll always care for her, but I've realized I'm no longer in love with her. Moving here made me realize that."

"Moving here?" she said, suddenly finding it hard to breathe.

He wrapped his arms around her again and murmured in her ear, "There's something very special about Heartsprings Valley. *Someone* very special."

"Someone?" she managed to whisper.

He gave her a mischievous grin. "You might know her. A wonderful woman named Holly Snow. Maybe you've met her?"

"Maybe I have," she said, blinking back a rush of tears.

"She's an incredible woman — smart and generous and hardworking and beautiful. She runs a terrific cafe on the town square — you should check it out sometime. She cares so much about her cafe and her employees and her family and her town."

"Is that so?" she said, blinking even faster.

"The instant I met her, I knew I was in trouble. Deep, serious, wonderful trouble. I felt lighter when I was with her. Her sense of purpose is so strong — along with her sense of fun." He squeezed her tighter. "And did I mention she's beautiful?"

Holly laughed. "You know, last night, when Carrie led you away, I thought…."

"I'm sorry about that," he said. "I hope I never again give you cause to doubt my intentions."

A feeling of assurance flowed through her as she accepted what that meant. The dream was actually happening. Her wishes were becoming real. With him — with this wonderful, caring man.

"Speaking of intentions," she said, waving her arm as she gazed upon the cafe's transformation. "How did you…?"

He chuckled. "A true team effort. When I couldn't reach you this morning —"

"I turned off my phone."

"I know." Pressing his cheek against hers, he whispered, very softly, "Very annoying of you, by the way."

She laughed. "I'm sorry. But I thought…."

"Oh, I totally get why. If the tables had been turned, I might have done the same. Of course, it did mean a rethink when I got to the cafe this morning and discovered you weren't here."

"A rethink?"

"You'd already gone home when I got back to the cafe last night. So I showed up here first thing to tell you that, despite Carrie's surprise appearance, nothing had changed for me."

"And when you found out I wasn't here, and that I was hiding under my covers...."

"I didn't find out about the cover-hiding right away. First I had to get through your team."

"Oh, really?"

"Let's just say Amanda was a bit, um, reserved. Polite and professional, of course, but, um...."

"Frosty?"

He chuckled. "I told her I needed to talk with you, and she told me I couldn't. When I asked why I couldn't talk with you, she said you weren't available. When I asked why you weren't available, she said you were taking the day off. When I asked where you'd gone on your day off, she told me she wasn't at liberty to say. Then she told me, very stiffly, that she wished me and Carrie the best of luck."

Holly grinned. Showing restraint like that must have been a struggle.

"George was a different story," he continued. "He marched right out of the kitchen and told me I was an idiot to let you go."

Holly laughed. *Dear, sweet, grumpy George.*

"So what did you do?"

"Well, my plan had been to tell you first, but when I realized that wasn't going to fly, I laid it all out. I told them that Carrie and I weren't getting back together, and that my plans hadn't changed, and that I didn't want to be an idiot."

She laughed again. "And?"

"When your mom showed up, the real team planning got under way."

"Who thought up doing this here?"

"Your mom. I wanted to go to your house right away, but she insisted that you'd prefer being dressed up a bit."

Holly smiled. "She was right about that. I was a mess." Her eyes landed on the red rose on the table. "The rose?"

"George."

"That's so sweet of him. The fire inspector story?"

"Amanda."

"The music, and lighting, and…?"

"All of us."

"You in a suit?"

"My idea." He leaned closer, his dark brown eyes locked on hers. "Dressed to impress."

"Mission accomplished," she said, pulling him tight.

His eyes became bright with emotion. "I'm so glad I moved to Heartsprings Valley. So grateful I met you."

Her eyes filled with tears. "Me, too."

"Merry Christmas, Holly."

"Merry Christmas, Gabe."

Then they kissed, their souls uniting, knowing that in each other they'd found their perfect match.

THE END

I DREAM OF CHRISTMAS

A HEARTSPRINGS VALLEY WINTER TALE
(BOOK 4)

Stuck in a storm with a handsome stranger!

Broadway singing star Melody Connelly is back
Heartsprings Valley and getting ready for a perfect
Christmas when she's caught in a fierce winter
storm with James, a handsome furniture craftsman.
Does Melody's perfect Christmas include a chance
at romance?

ALSO BY ANNE CHASE

AVAILABLE NOW OR COMING SOON

Heartsprings Valley Romances

Christmas to the Rescue!

A Very Cookie Christmas

Sweet Apple Christmas

I Dream of Christmas

Chock Full of Christmas

The Christmas Sleuth

Eagle Cove Mysteries

Murder So Deep

Murder So Cold

Murder So Pretty

Murder So Tender

Emily Livingston Mysteries

A Death in Barcelona

From Rome, With Murder

Paris Is for Killers

In London We Die

A heartwarming holiday story about a handsome veterinarian and the shy, beautiful librarian he meets on Christmas Eve....

Nick and the Snowplow is a companion to *Christmas to the Rescue!*, the first novel in the Heartsprings Valley Winter Tale series. In *Christmas to the Rescue!*, a young librarian named Becca gets caught in a blizzard on Christmas Eve, finds shelter with a handsome veterinarian named Nick, and ends up experiencing the most surprising, adventure-filled night of her life.

Nick and the Snowplow, told from Nick's point of view, shows what happens after Nick brings Becca home at the end of their whirlwind evening.

This story is available FOR FREE when you sign up for Anne Chase's email newsletter.

Go to AnneChase.com to sign up and get your free story.

ABOUT THE AUTHOR

Greetings! I grew up in a small town (pop: 2,000) and now live in the bustling Bay Area. I write romances and mysteries, including:

The *Heartsprings Valley* romances: Celebrating love at Christmas in a small New England town.

The *Eagle Cove Mysteries:* An inquisitive cafe owner gets dragged into in murder and mayhem.

The *Emily Livingston Mysteries:* Intrigue and danger amidst the glamour and beauty of Europe.

My email newsletter is a great way to find out about upcoming books. Go to **AnneChase.com** to sign up.

Thank you for being a reader!

Printed in Great Britain
by Amazon